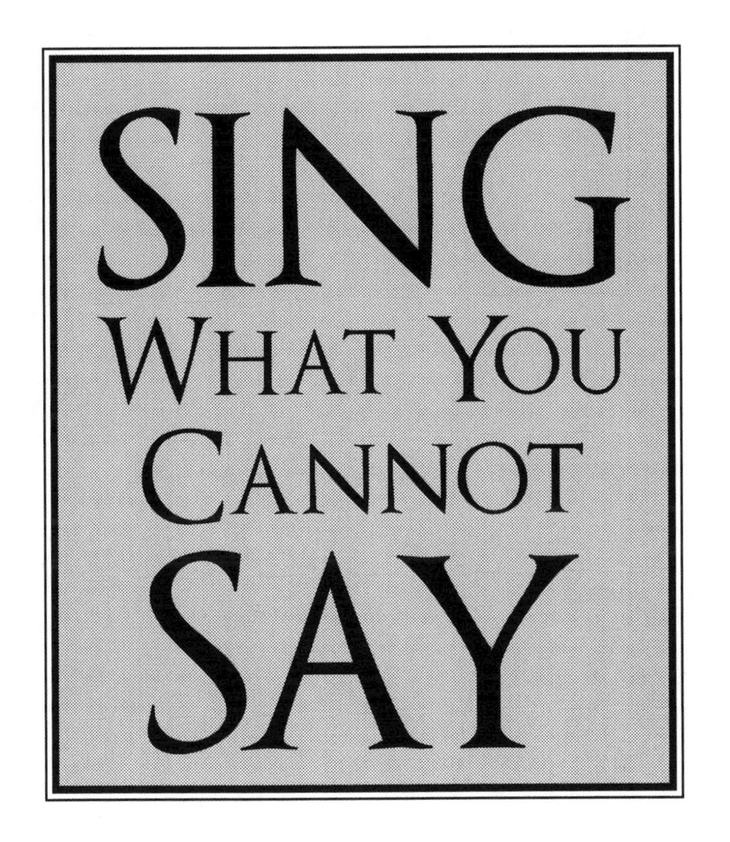

Cathy Raymond

SING WHAT YOU CANNOT SAY

This is a work of fiction. All of the characters, names, incidents, organizations, and dialogue in this novel are either the products of the author's imagination or are used fictitiously.

iUniverse books may be ordered through booksellers or by contacting:

iUniverse
1663 Liberty Drive
Bloomington, IN 47403
www.iuniverse.com
1-800-Authors (1-800-288-4677)

ISBN: 978-1-4917-6405-3 (sc)
ISBN: 978-1-4917-6406-0 (e)

Library of Congress Control Number: 2015907671

Print information available on the last page.

iUniverse rev. date: 06/17/2015

To the musicians and composers who bravely strived to maintain their dignity while also offering hope to others during the most unimaginable times.

One

January 1942

As she flipped onto her side, Anna could hear the wind howling outside the barracks. The worn blanket did little to cover her and even less to keep her thin body from shivering. It had been three months since Anna Katz had arrived in Terezin from Prague. Life there had become all but unbearable. They were no longer allowed to own property or even go to concerts, and all of them now had to wear the star.

Anna thought she had found a way out of Prague, but initial promises that she and her family would be brought to safety—they had been told that Terezin was a new Jewish city where they could live comfortably and safely—had been quickly replaced by three-tiered bunks and two square yards per person for cooking, sleeping, and bathroom facilities. Terezin was clearly no Jewish settlement. It was a concentration camp.

Anna rolled onto her back and stared at the ceiling as she slowly hummed the first line of a Czech lullaby her mother had sung to her as a child. "Spi, detatko, spi …" Sleep, child, sleep. She took care to keep her voice low, so the guards wouldn't be disturbed. A quiet voice joined her own and then another. Layers of sound; melody, harmony—quiet courage.

Her stomach rumbled, and she wrapped her arms around her middle to quiet the sound. She would have to switch to her other side soon; her bony hips offered little padding against the hard, thin mattress.

The door flew open, and in came a burst of icy air from the winter night. The light switched on suddenly. "Who is that singing?"

Everyone kept still as the guard walked from bunk to bunk. He stopped at Anna's bed and poked her back with a stick. "Is that you singing?"

Anna kept her eyes closed and quietly replied, "Yes, sir."

He tore the blanket from her and ordered her to get up. "I thought it might be you. Come with me. *Now.*" The guard quickly marched toward the door. Anna had no choice but to follow him into the cold night.

* * *

Two

January 2014

Emily taught her usual courses that week—Introduction to Contemporary Music, German Expressionist Composers, and A Survey of Western Music. It was a heavy load by any standard, and she had had little time to prepare for the upcoming midweek conference on "Music during the Nazi Period." As she finished up her last lecture for the week, she thought with apprehension about her presentation on Felix Steinitz and his musical writings from the concentration camp Terezin. At this point she still only had a jumbled mess of dates and facts—precisely the type of thing that turned people away from learning about history. She realized with a sinking feeling that she'd have to spend her Friday evening in her office and not at the new French restaurant Chez Nous with her boyfriend, Brian, so she could weave the details of Steinitz's life and work into a captivating story. She had a feeling Brian would not be happy. He didn't like any changes to his schedule, especially if he lost out to Emily's work.

Emily flipped up the collar of the thin jacket she was wearing and picked up her pace as she made her way across campus and back to her office. A sudden icy blast of air made her gasp; her lungs ached from the cold, and she felt around her pocket to make sure she had her inhaler. She wondered briefly, as she often did during the winter months, if her California friends had been right. They had warned her that life in Wisconsin would be intolerable; the winters were harsh and the summers were short. She had ignored them and jumped into her new position with gratitude and excitement over having a job in a tough economy, especially in her chosen field.

As she made her way across campus, she thought about her boyfriend, Brian. They had been seeing each other for ten months. Although her friends in California had not openly told her what they thought of him, she could sense their surprise that the relationship had lasted so long. She herself liked to believe that she needed someone different from her usual type; he worked as an optometrist and had a life as regular as the mail. He could always say when he would be home from work, where he would be at lunch and dinner (oftentimes even what he would eat for lunch and dinner), and where he would be on the weekend. Emily sometimes even secretly wondered if his trips to the bathroom were scheduled. His life was like a chant: breakfast at seven, lunch at noon, work until five. Brian told Emily he loved the feeling that the day was divided by clear boundaries of work and free time.

Brian's rigid attitudes about life scheduling sometimes drove Emily nuts, but she was also convinced that she had finally broken her own pattern and had found someone good for her for once—different from her usual type. Seven years earlier, she had fallen for Chris, an artist who worked on his paintings in the middle of the night, slept all day, and regularly disappeared for days on end. At that time she'd found herself playing the waiting game until, after two years of constant yearning, she'd finally built a protective wall and told herself it didn't matter. Just in time for him to find another artist like himself. He had actually used the words *soul mate* to describe his new girlfriend when he broke up with Emily.

Then she had promptly met Harry. He was a lawyer who worked long hours and was so obsessed with his clients and work that she'd only seen him when she'd agreed to put on formal wear and accompany him to gala fundraisers and client dinners. Their relationship had ended when she'd gotten the job offer from the music history department at the University of Wisconsin in Madison. Before they could even discuss the offer, Harry quickly had broken it off, citing impatience with the pragmatic challenges of relationship negotiation. He'd said there was no chance it could ever work with him in California and her in Wisconsin.

Emily had decided that the move to Madison was her chance for a clean break. She could start fresh and leave her troubled past relationships behind. And with a new professor's hectic schedule, she'd managed to avoid anything but short-term relationships for the first five years. Brian had broken her record; she had immediately been drawn to his sense of regularity and had been convinced that he was a welcome change to her usual pattern. Maybe this was a man she could finally depend on.

Her own life couldn't be more different from Brian's. Her schedule changed virtually every week and left her resembling a ping-pong ball bouncing from one irregularly scheduled obligation to the next. She rarely ate breakfast (mainly because she routinely ignored her morning alarm and was left with only a few minutes to shower, dress, pack her bag, and run out the door). She worked lunch in when it was convenient, which meant she frequently found herself starving by three o'clock, and sometimes didn't even start her own research until five o'clock. She thrived on unpredictability—the central aspect of her career. She darted from one activity to the next, rushing through the hallways to get to her next assignment, immersing herself in a new research topic, and preparing for teaching and presentations.

Brian's predictable nature was a blessing and a curse; he kept her sane when her own life spiraled, but he also drove her crazy when he refused to budge from his routine. She knew that she could also frustrate him with her spontaneous nature and irregular schedule. It was amazing their relationship had lasted ten months.

As she finally let herself into her office, she made a mental note to buy a thicker coat in the morning—maybe even one of those crazy down numbers that went below the knees. She chuckled in spite of herself as she thought of her California friends and their certain I-told-you-sos.

Emily rubbed her hands together briskly to warm them. She reached for the phone and slowly drew in a breath. She dialed and mentally counted the rings—Brian was sure to pick up after number three. She decided to cut to the chase when she heard his voice on the other end of the phone.

"Hi, it's me. I'm afraid I have a bit of unexpected bad news. I was planning on working on my presentation today, but I had no time at all. I'm afraid I'll have to—"

Brian cut her off. "Work through the weekend? Really, Em?"

Emily squeezed her eyes shut, breathed in slowly, and counted to three before answering. "Brian, I'm sorry, but—"

"I thought we had agreed to spend the evening together—no work. Couldn't you have planned ahead a little more? Just this once?"

Emily felt her belly tighten, and she went into self-defensive mode. "Bri, I know we had plans for tonight, but it's not like I intended to sabotage our evening together. I did try to tell you this might happen. My teaching schedule is so crazy this semester, and I—"

Brian interrupted her again. "This kind of thing seems to happen a lot with you. What's the big deal anyway? Didn't you just go to a conference last month? Why is this conference so important anyway? Don't you *want* a private life?"

Emily had known this conversation was going to be difficult, but surely Brian must understand her need to get work done? She took a deep breath and slowly replied, "Brian, you know how important publications are for my tenure review. This conference is a shoo-in for getting my manuscript noticed."

"Tenure, tenure, that's all you talk about."

Brian clearly had no idea what hoops she had to jump through just to keep her job. Emily breathed in deeply and forced out the words she had practiced in front of a mirror many times. "This is my work. I take it very seriously, and it's a major part of who I am. If I want to keep this job, this is what I have to do."

"Yes, yes, I know, but I don't always want to play second fiddle."

"What are you saying?"

"I'm saying I want a girlfriend who wants what I want."

"Which is what exactly?"

"A life."

Emily heard a click, and she slowly set the receiver back in its cradle. So much for speaking her mind. All those hours at the therapist for what? She felt a pang of guilt as she gathered her papers and moved to her work space. This was going to be a long night …

Before diving into writing, Emily braced the cold one final time and dashed out to Sam's Sandwich Parlor for a pastrami on rye sandwich and an extra-large cup of coffee. It was no beef bourguignon, but for some unknown reason, a pastrami on rye had always helped her concentrate.

It was her writer's inspiration. A pastrami on rye was also a sign to the outside world that she was in the middle of an important project. (Colleagues envious of her success had even tried the formula for themselves, but to no avail. The P-on-R formula worked only for Emily.)

Making her way to the deli, Emily began to doubt her sense of judgment and wondered if ordering a pizza for delivery might not have been a better idea after all. Now that the sun had set, the icy wind took on a new, almost menacing, quality. She stuffed her hands into her pockets and reminded herself again to go to Burlington Coat Factory in the morning to try on down coats. And mittens. And most definitely hats.

Once her appetite was sated, Emily headed back to her office. She could hear her cell phone ringing as she unlocked her door—it was Brian's ring tone from the Mozart Requiem. She had set the ringer to the Requiem after their first major fight eight months earlier and hadn't gotten around to switching it back. She hummed along to the Sanctus chorus as she dug through her bag to find the phone. She caught the call just before it flipped to voice mail.

"Hey," she said quietly.

"Hey, Emily, about that earlier call …"

"I'm sorry, Brian. I know you were looking forward to a quiet evening together, and I'm really—"

"No, Emily, I am sorry. I had no right to criticize you. You work so hard all the time. It's amazing you even have time to eat."

Emily felt another sharp pang of guilt as she thought about her sandwich.

Brian continued, "I know that I am rigid in my ways, and we have quite different approaches to life, but I'd like to make this work. I just wanted to say that."

Maybe the therapy was paying dividends after all. "I would like to try to make this work too. I wish I could say that getting tenure was easier, but there are a lot of hoops to jump through before I'll be considered. I've had almost six years to prove myself, and I'm on the final push."

"I'm gonna try harder to understand that, Em. I guess my job is just a little more straightforward. I do a good job, I keep my job. Simple formula."

Emily smiled. "Some people say the tenure process should be completely done away with for a lot of reasons. One of those reasons is the toll it takes on relationships." Emily paused briefly before continuing. "Brian, we are very different people, but you know what they say about opposites attracting."

"I'm glad you see it my way, Em. So are you going to sleep at the office, or could you come by when you're done working and stop for a drink?"

"A drink sounds fabulous."

"By the way, what are you even writing about? I'm embarrassed to say I forgot to even ask."

"The conference is on the Holocaust, and I'm going to talk about a composer—his name was Felix Steinitz. He was in a concentration camp and managed to continue writing music the entire time he was there."

"What exactly are you going to talk about?"

Emily breathed out slowly. "Are you really interested in this, or are you just trying to squeeze a little date in now after all?"

"A bit of both, I guess."

"Let's talk more over a glass of wine later. It'll be much nicer to talk in person."

"Agreed."

Emily said good-bye and hung up. She turned the thermometer up to seventy-five to blast the room with heat. Then she looked at the mess of papers on her desk. If she was going to complete her article by Sunday, she needed absolute clarity of thought. She didn't really want to take the time to sort through all the papers on her desk, but they were distracting. She quickly decided to shove all the papers to both sides of her desk, clearing a path down the middle. A clear stretch of wood opened up down the center, and she immediately felt her energy level rising. She hadn't had time to write in weeks, and she was really looking forward to it. And Emily loved to wait until the sun had gone down before she did her writing. When it was dark, she could really concentrate. No one would knock on her door; the phone wouldn't ring. It was just Emily, the dark, and her thoughts.

She reviewed the notes she had made from sketches of an opera Felix Steinitz had written in the concentration camp Terezin. She had gathered a lot of fascinating material from archives and wanted to continue her mission of making Steinitz as well-known as possible.

Emily started sketching out her presentation. She would begin with background information on the camp Terezin. She wondered how much conference participants would know about the camps, Terezin in particular, and she needed to include at least some basic background information before moving to her presentation of Steinitz's work. She looked out the window at the trees and thought how the purpose of Terezin had been a bit different from the other camps the Nazis had established. The Nazis had decided they needed a "model" camp to fool the world into believing that the Jews were being resettled to a safe place. Ironically, the plan had been to tell the world that Hitler had built a safe haven city for the Jews to protect them from the misery and destruction of the war. Terezin had been chosen as this city, and much effort had been put into portraying it as a settlement camp. The Nazis had even gone on to make a propaganda movie to convince the outside world that the Jews had everything they could ever want or need.

The harsh reality was that thousands of people had died in Terezin, and thousands more had been deported to extermination camps like Auschwitz and Treblinka.

Emily grimaced when she thought about the ironic term *settlement*; there had been little that was "settled" about Terezin, as it was primarily meant as a temporary stopping point for prisoners on the way to the other extermination camps.

Emily wanted people to understand that Terezin had been intended in many ways as a propaganda camp to fool Western allies into believing that the Jews had everything they needed, while also allowing the Nazis to boast publicly that Terezin had a rich cultural community. The Nazis had focused on three main groups of German, Austrian, and Czech Jews when they'd set up Terezin: those who were "too old" to work, veterans of the First World War, and Jews who might have raised suspicion if they went missing because they were sufficiently well-known. Emily paused to reflect on the cunning of the Nazis who had needed, and then created, a place to hold the famous musicians and artists whose disappearances might have caused alarm in the international community. Ironically, it was also for this reason that Terezin had had such a vibrant and active musical life.

Emily felt a jolt when her office phone rang. She glanced at her watch. Midnight. She reached over her papers to pick up the phone.

"Yes, hello?" Emily asked quickly, expecting a wrong number.

The voice on the other end of the line hesitated. "Uh … Ms. Thurgood?"

"Yes, this is she. Who am I speaking to please?"

"Uh, Ms. Thurgood, I don't know if you remember me. We met at a party about four months ago—uh, my name is Harold Hansen."

Emily's mind was still on Terezin, so it took her a second to place the name. A face gradually formed in her mind, and she responded slowly, "Well, uh … yes, Mr. Hansen. You … uh … work at the university library if I remember correctly."

Harold Hansen's noticeable sigh seemed to fill Emily's office. "Oh, good, you do remember me. I was afraid you wouldn't. I'm sure you meet so many new people at parties and things."

Emily reached for her cigarettes. She had technically quit three months before, but writing always made her itch for a smoke. "Mr. Hansen, it's a bit late for a chat, don't you think? Any reason you needed to call me at this time of night? You do know what time it is, right?"

"Well, I'd, uh …" Emily heard papers rustling in the background. "I'd like to meet with you and talk about it in person if that's possible. I have something you might be interested in seeing. It might be important. Could we possibly meet sometime tomorrow?"

Emily took a quick drag on her cigarette. "What do you have to show me that warrants a midnight call?"

Hansen cleared his throat. "I really do apologize for calling so late. I tried earlier, but I couldn't reach you at home. I only now thought of calling you at your office. A lot of professors seem to like working late, so I thought I'd see if you were in. I really wouldn't have bothered you, but I think you'll forgive me once you see what I have to show you."

Emily's curiosity was piqued, but she needed to stay on track with her preparation. "This all sounds very mysterious, but unfortunately I'm in the middle of preparing an important presentation and need most of the weekend for it. I have a conference next week, and my schedule is completely booked. Could we maybe meet in a week when I am back from the conference—say, on Monday? That's really my first available opening. I am sorry, but things are always a bit tight before a conference."

Hansen didn't answer immediately. Emily heard some papers rustling in the background again. "Well, uh … if that's really the only possibility, then I guess it'll have to wait. How about Monday morning in a week at ten o'clock in the library? Is that possible for you?"

"It's on my calendar. Good night." Emily slowly hung up the phone. What on earth did Hansen want? And why did he need to call on Friday at midnight? And what could he possibly have to show her that was so important? A strange sensation tugged at her, and she wondered if she should have agreed to meet with him sooner.

As she drove to Brian's house an hour later, Hansen's call preoccupied Emily. *Maybe I should just meet with him this weekend*, she reasoned. *What could he possibly want to show me?* A small voice objected, *Oh no you don't. If you let yourself get sidetracked this weekend, you'll never finish your article. Just put it out of your mind for now. Hansen can wait until Monday. If it were that important, he would have insisted on meeting this weekend, right?*

The voices fought with each other the entire ride. And in the end, sensibility won. The conference was simply too important to jeopardize. If she didn't devote her entire weekend to the presentation, she would never be ready. *There*, she thought. *It's all settled. I'll have a glass of wine with Brian, grab a couple of hours of sleep, and spend the rest of the weekend working on my paper. And tomorrow I will unplug the phone in my office. Then I won't make any calls, and no one will call me.*

Emily pulled into Brian's driveway knowing she would now sleep easily and deeply. She wouldn't need much sleep either. Exciting projects always gave her an added boost and let her get by on four or five hours a night. She felt fortunate to have been blessed with such an agreeable sleep system. Most of her colleagues needed at least eight hours a night—regardless of their schedules. But then again, they took less time for class preparation and more time for their own work during the semester. They didn't need to compensate for lost time.

Brian's light was still on, and Emily knocked on the door.

"Well, look what the cat dragged in. I thought you had decided to sleep at work after all," Brian said.

Emily gave Brian a quick kiss on the cheek. "Sorry it's so late, hon. I'm glad you are still awake. I brought this." Emily held up a bottle of California Merlot. If she was honest, she had to admit that she was missing the warmth of California right about now. The bottle of wine had beckoned to her from the shelf in the store where she bought her cigarettes.

Brian pulled Emily into his arms and kissed her warmly. "You can't get away with a peck on the cheek, Em. I need a real hug." Emily could smell Irish Spring on his neck as they embraced. Brian whispered in her ear, "Look, I'm sorry about earlier. I was just really looking forward to some time together. Thanks for coming by now."

One bottle of wine later, the conversation had drifted to Emily's presentation. Brian leaned over and touched Emily's arm. "So tell me about this composer you're writing about."

"Are you sure you're interested? It's almost four in the morning."

"Of course. You're writing about an opera, right? I am interested, but I'm not a huge fan of opera. Just don't hold it against me if I start falling asleep!"

Emily smiled. "It's actually standard opera stuff. It's about a king who rules with an iron fist. He is Napoleonic in his quest for land and power."

Brian said, "That sounds surprisingly like Hitler. Didn't you say this was during World War II?"

Emily sipped on her wine. "Yes, exactly. That's part of what's so interesting about this. Steinitz makes it appear as though he is presenting the king in a positive light."

Brian yawned. "Why is that such a big deal?"

"Well, on a superficial level, the story line and the characters all seem fairly straightforward, but on a deeper musical level, there's a lot more going on."

Brian put up his hand. "Emily, you're gonna lose me on this part. Remember—I am a pretty literal guy. I don't do symbolism—and I'm exhausted."

Emily laughed. "It's actually really easy to understand, and I think you'll be intrigued. I'll keep it short and simple; I promise. It's the harmonies and melodies that are so interesting in the opera. I tore the thing apart and figured out that each character is musically marked by a motif or melody. The appearance of any given character is repeatedly signaled by an accompanying musical motif." Emily paused. "Are you with me so far?"

"Kind of like a theme song for each character?"

Emily nodded. "Exactly like that. And that's just the beginning. Tightly woven in the tapestry of Steinitz's music are quotes from well-known German pieces. And these melodies and fragments are by no means innocent. At the risk of death, the composer Felix Steinitz ironically manipulated these melodies and phrases in an attempt to criticize the Nazis covertly. He knew that virtually every ear in the world tied the melody of the German national anthem to Hitler and his barbaric plans. Every film, every newsreel on Hitler and Germany, every piece of propaganda at least briefly quoted the anthem. It literally became Hitler's theme song." She stopped and looked at Brian to see if he had fallen asleep yet.

Brian leaned closer. "Don't stop there. I don't get why it would have been dangerous to link Hitler with the national anthem."

Emily raised her eyebrows and leaned forward. "Ah ... Well, in his opera Steinitz disguised the quotes from the German national anthem, linking it to the tyrannical king and, by *secret* association, with Hitler. Each time the king made an appearance, a fragment of the first line of the anthem could be heard. But this fragment was not the blatant version of *'Deutschland, Deutschland über alles'* but rather its ironic inversion. Steinitz brilliantly began with the last note of the first line and simply reversed the order of the notes. To the untrained ear, it was nothing more than a harmless melody meant to identify the king. In reality it was a bold and courageous statement. The now-altered anthem was a parody of the original. Where the original national anthem would have immediately linked the metaphorical king to his more-than-real counterpart Hitler, the inversion of the powerful melody simultaneously rendered both impotent."

Brian's eyes were wide. "And the Nazis didn't figure that out?"

Emily shook her head. "Surprisingly, no. The other interesting thing is that the prisoners were tuned in to what was going on—no pun intended! Unfortunately, there aren't many survivors still alive today, but I was lucky enough to have a chance to talk to a couple of them last summer. In a way the prisoners were holding their captors captive."

Brian held his hand over his mouth to cover a yawn. "Sorry, Em. I just know your presentation's gonna be great, but right now I really need to hit the hay. I'm not used to staying up so late."

* * *

THREE

January 1942

Anna followed the guard to the main camp building. Even though it was midnight, bright lights illuminated the path. As they approached a small building, the guard shoved Anna through an open door, and she gasped. Nearly fifteen prisoners were lined up in three rows. Anna was told to join the women on the right side. She saw her good friend Lexa, who had arrived in Terezin just a month before. She stood next to her now and gently took her hand. She saw that the guard was holding a rifle, so she closed her eyes and started to pray silently.

The guard stood in front of the group, raised his rifle toward them, and ordered them to sing.

No one moved. Anna opened her eyes just a little and blinked. The guard was shifting his weight from foot to foot, and there was a bead of sweat on his forehead. He pointed the rifle at Anna. "You! I know you have studied music. Sing that song you were singing when I came into your cabin."

All eyes were on Anna. She turned to look at the other prisoners, and their eyes pleaded with her to do whatever it took to get them through the night.

She started singing softly. "Spi, detatko, spi …"

"All of you. *All* of you!" The guard was waving his rifle around frantically. The others slowly joined in until there was a full chorus of voices. Anna closed her eyes again as she sang and let herself imagine her mother's voice, her mother's hand stroking her forehead, brushing the hair back from her eyes …

When Anna opened her eyes, the guard was nodding and smiling. "Yes, that will do just fine. You are now all members of the new choir of Terezin." He waved his rifle toward the door. "Go back to bed. Report back here after your day's work duty, and we'll find some more-suitable German songs for the choir."

* * *

Four

January 2014

Brian was fiddling with his coffee spoon as Emily shuffled around the kitchen at ten o'clock the next morning. "Em, there's a great movie playing today. Maybe we could hit the matinee at one o'clock?"

Emily ran her fingers through her hair and looked down to avoid Brian's eyes. "I really wish I could, but I've got to stay on track with my presentation. I'm already exhausted from our long night. If I don't spend the day working, I'll never get through this thing. I better take a rain check."

Suddenly remembering Hansen's call, and not wanting to get into another argument, Emily quickly changed the topic. "By the way, I got a very strange call last night from someone I met at a party a few months ago. Do you remember a Harold Hansen? The librarian? He was at Susan's party a while back. I talked to him for quite some time at the party. Apparently, he's got something really important to show me, but he couldn't tell me about it on the phone. It must be pretty important—he called at midnight."

Brian stopped toying with his spoon. "What is it he wanted?"

"That's just it," Emily said slowly. "I really don't know. He insisted on talking to me in person, and he said he had something to show me, so we arranged to meet a week from Monday once the conference is over. I must admit, I'm very curious. But I promised myself on the way over here last night that I wouldn't give in and call him back today. I just can't afford the time this weekend. It'll have to wait. It's probably nothing anyway."

Something was nagging at Emily, but she decided to attribute it to nerves. The conference deadline must be getting to her.

She stood up. "I've really got to get back to work. I'll call you later this afternoon, okay? What are you going to do today? Do you have any plans?" She regretted the question the second it slipped out.

"Well, I was really hoping we could have some time together this weekend, but I see that's not gonna happen. I guess I'll go over to my sister's later on and watch some football with her and Rick. Other than that, I'll probably just hang out here. Maybe I'll toy around with the computer or play fix-it man and see if I can get the dishwasher working again."

Emily was grateful that Brian hadn't taken the opportunity to pick a new fight. She grabbed her coat and headed for the door. "That sounds great, hon. Say hello to Ann and Rick for me. If I don't reach you here, I'll try you there later today. Have a great day." She left quickly, remembering only later that she had forgotten to kiss Brian good-bye.

Driving to the university, Emily switched on the radio. She heard the first strains of Rachmaninov's Second Piano Concerto and began whistling along energetically. Over the years Emily had developed the habit of whistling to piano music whenever she heard it. She had grown up with classical music—her mother and father were both concert pianists who also taught at the university—and somewhere along the way she had picked up the habit of accompanying them like a bird whenever they played. Gradually it became such second nature that Emily only rarely noticed when her whistle kicked in. One of those times had been her first meeting with Brian.

Unbeknownst to Emily, Brian also had the daily habit of eating lunch at the Village Deli. (It had been one of the few predictable moments in Emily's day back then.) For months Emily had eaten lunch at the same place, but she had never noticed Brian.

One day when Emily had been waiting for her pastrami on rye (she was working on a big project at the time), the soothing tones of Schumann's Träumerei had floated through the room. Emily's high-pitched whistle had accompanied the pianist.

Emily had been completely oblivious to her birdlike warble. It had glided, soared, trilled, gently swayed, and gracefully carried Schumann's melody throughout the entire restaurant.

Suddenly she'd had the feeling that everyone was staring at her. As she'd looked up from her newspaper, she'd seen Brian sitting at the next table. He had been smiling at her, and she'd asked him what was so funny.

"Nothing," Brian had said smiling. "I've just never heard such a beautiful whistle before, and I wanted to make sure you didn't have a bird under your table."

Emily had been mortified. "Oh my God. Was I whistling? How embarrassing." She'd quickly surveyed the restaurant, only to find that all eyes were on her. "Oh, I wish I could just disappear. Damn whistle anyway. I picked that up as a child, and it sort of kicks in automatically whenever I hear piano music. Thanks for saving me. I never would have noticed."

She'd surprised herself by spontaneously inviting Brian to join her for lunch. Normally she would have been too shy to do so, but she had been immediately struck by Brian's smile. It had been so natural and full. And he was obviously a very curious person—a trait Emily adored in people. Anyone with the nerve to approach a whistling, raving lunatic in a restaurant was worth getting to know.

Before the Rachmaninov concerto had ended, Emily was already pulling her car into the parking lot. *Typical*, she thought, *now I'll have to sit in the cold car until the piece is over. Why can't they play shorter pieces when I drive to work?* Emily turned off the car, leaned back, and whistled with the pianist to the end of the concerto.

As the announcer's voice filled the car, Emily quickly turned off the radio and opened the car door. Before she got pulled into the next piece of music, she wanted to escape to her safe office. She had to be careful not to procrastinate too much. Even the radio could be dangerous.

Emily locked herself in her office, unplugged the phone, and worked without interruption for the next six hours. In that time, she managed to finish the bulk of her presentation. She would finish the conclusion and follow-up remarks that evening and Sunday. In the meantime, she would go see if Brian wanted to grab a bite to eat.

By the time Emily reached Brian, he had fixed the dishwasher, watched the Green Bay Packers win their third game out of three, and done something mysterious with the computer that he was pretty pleased about. Emily was personally unimpressed with the details of a computer's innards, but Brian was always poking around computer parts and rebuilding his machine every few months. Emily preferred poring over old, faded manuscripts. History came alive for her when she had a really old document in her hands. She could almost see a composer at work, pencil in hand, head bowed over paper. A computer held little mystery for her. It was simply a means to an end—a way to get her next article into print.

Emily was thrilled, though, that Brian had clearly adjusted well to spending the day alone. "I promise we'll do something fun after the conference. Thanks for being so patient with me." She reached for his arm and pulled him close, giving him a warm kiss on the lips.

Brian hugged her tightly and whispered in her ear, "Maybe a football game?"

Emily laughed loudly. She was no fan of the sport, but she wanted to treat him for being so patient, so she agreed. "Why don't you see if you can get tickets for a game? I'd love that."

Brian held Emily at arm's length and looked her directly in the eye. "Really? Are you serious, Em? That would be so awesome!"

"Yes, I'm serious! But now I really need to get back to the grindstone."

The rest of the evening flew by. After another abbreviated night's sleep, she was sitting at her desk by seven the next morning. Sunday was Saturday's twin, and by midnight the presentation was more or less finished. She straightened her desk for the busy week ahead and turned off the light.

* * *

The full moon lit the parking lot, and a cold January breeze brushed across Emily's face. She thought about Steinitz and his hope, his indomitable passion for music and life, his courage in the face of barbed wire and Nazi terror. She felt a rush a gratitude for her own comfortable life, the gift of her career, her boyfriend, her freedom. She considered the irony of fate and history. What had placed her in such a time of comfort, while Steinitz—with all his talents and courage—had landed in a place of unfathomable despair? She thought about a poem by Bertolt Brecht she had memorized in graduate school, "To Those Born After." Brecht's poem perfectly described how random life was—how the elements of chance and fate decided under which circumstances we were born and lived, and how those unique circumstances directed the path our lives would take.

Emily felt the tears welling up as she slowly recited Brecht's poem. Steinitz's creative genius and his courage filled her with conviction to make him known to the world. He had passed through this world as a beacon of hope, and she was determined to see his works played and sung by orchestras and choirs all over the world.

As she always did when she drove, Emily turned on the radio. Soothing music filled the car, and she felt her mind shifting gears. The tension of the entire weekend and the fear that she wouldn't finish her presentation gradually left her body. She felt relaxed. Schubert, Bach, and Chopin—her longtime favorite composers. She let her mind drift with the melodies.

The radio announcer introduced the next piece, and Emily reached over to turn off the radio. It wasn't a piece she knew, and she was afraid to jeopardize the calmness she was feeling. Music she had never heard before was too exciting—it made her listen too closely. And she wanted to be able to sleep when she got home.

But before Emily could switch off the radio, a single haunting melody filled the car. Solo piano. Emily was hypnotized. Her ear eagerly followed the pianist's right hand as it slowly wound its way across the keyboard. Gradually the left hand entered. The emerging harmonies were piercingly lonely. Suddenly, a dominant rhythm took over the melody, and the mood shifted. It was a strong, independent pulse that demanded Emily's complete attention.

She absently drove into Brian's driveway and turned off the car. She left the radio on and didn't move. As the piece gradually came to a close, the porch light came on, and Brian came outside. "What are you doing out there in the car? It's past midnight and freezing! Come inside, or you'll catch a cold." Emily waved to Brian from inside the car, motioning from her ears and back to the radio that she was listening to something and would be in shortly. She wanted to wait until the end of the piece, to hear who the composer was, before she went inside.

Brian was walking toward the car, but Emily held up her hand to keep him at bay while the announcer read the name of the composer. He was young—unknown. Emily listened attentively and made a mental note of the name. She popped open the car door and saw that Brian had gone back into the house.

As she went inside, Brian was waiting with a glass of wine. He handed her the glass and made a toast. "For the hardest-working music historian in Wisconsin. May she have a wonderful conference. By the way, what on earth were you doing in the car? Spacing out to music again?"

Emily laughed and took the glass from Brian's hand. "Sorry it took me so long to come in. I had to listen to the end of a new piano piece. Hauntingly beautiful. Truly a testament to the power of music to feed the soul. I'll have to find out what else this Henry Cramer has written."

* * *

FIVE

January 1943

Terezin felt more and more cramped and crowded as each day passed. It was clear to Anna that the camp had never been meant to house more than seven thousand people, but now tens of thousands were cramming its every corner. Food was being rationed, and all around her Anna saw people starving or dying every day from the many illnesses at the camp. Rats, fleas, and lice were everywhere.

If the everyday life conditions weren't hard enough, the prisoners were also assigned to long hours of work each day. Some of them had to stand in makeshift assembly lines, ironically to make items for the German war effort. Others were forced to haul rock or dig in the dirt all day in freezing temperatures. Some had to peel potatoes for hours at a time or scrub giant pots that had been filled with a watery soup. Trained artists and mathematicians were made to keep detailed reports for the SS on what was happening in the camp. Simple mistakes like a typo or a minor error in addition could lead to harsh punishment or even to death.

Music would never make the increasingly harsh realities of life in Terezin disappear, but Anna knew from experience that it could give her and the others courage and hope. She often had little or no food, and sleep was hard to come by on a thin mattress and an empty stomach. But she found the energy for music and song. It was the one thing left that no one could take from her. The women in her choir group often said they could not sing because they were hungry. She told them every day that they had to sing *because* they were hungry. It was food for their souls.

Felix Steinitz had also recently arrived in Terezin, so they were not only singing every day; the overall quality of the music at the camp had improved significantly. Steinitz had been well known to Anna when she had been studying at the Prague Conservatory, and now he was actually here at Terezin. He had made vocal arrangements of Hebrew and Yiddish folk songs for them to sing each evening, and she had heard he was even composing an opera! Anna felt stronger with Steinitz and his music nearby.

Rafael Schächter had also recently arrived at the camp, and under his direction, Anna and the choir had begun rehearsing Verdi's Requiem. Anna had met Schächter at the Prague Conservatory, where they had both studied music composition. Schächter enlisted Anna's help now. Her job was to help him by coaching the women with the music and the Latin text from Verdi's Requiem while Schächter helped the men. There was only one copy of Verdi's Requiem for 150 singers. It was a momentous task, but they would all have to learn each line of music and each line of Latin text by heart.

Learning the text and preparing for the performance of Verdi's Requiem were the only things that distracted Anna from the daily trains that pulled away from Terezin carrying friends and loved ones eastward.

* * *

Six

January 2014

The week got off to a flying start, and Emily knew she wouldn't be seeing much of Brian that week. One of the other optometrists was sick with the flu, and Brian had to jump in for her at the last minute. And Emily's week was going to be short; she only had Monday and Tuesday to get everything done before her drive to Chicago on Wednesday. Those two days were filled with frazzled students, committee meetings, and last-minute changes to her presentation. It seemed Emily had just gotten out of bed when it was time for her to head off to the conference.

"You'll be fine. You are so good. Everyone is always so eager to hear what you have to say." Emily always got nervous before conferences, and she was grateful to Brian for trying to get her to relax.

"Thanks, Bri," Emily said, "but somehow I feel like I forgot something important or that I should have approached the material differently. Do you think I'm getting unnecessarily nervous?"

Emily felt a reassuring squeeze on her shoulder. "Absolutely. You always get nervous right before a conference, and then everything is fine in the end. I have faith in you."

Emily reached over and massaged the back of Brian's neck. "Bri, I appreciate how patient you have been the last couple of weeks. I've been a pain lately, but I'll make it up to you when I get back—I promise."

The drive to Chicago passed quickly. Emily settled into her hotel and reviewed her notes. Her pre-presentation anxiety set in, and she reminded herself to focus on Steinitz's courage and passion.

Two hours later, Emily was introduced to a crowded room of historians. She took her place at the podium and began to talk about Steinitz. Once she started talking, her nervousness was replaced by the strong desire to disseminate every piece of hidden history she had uncovered. She could think only of Steinitz, his music, and the conditions under which he and many other composers had lived, worked, and created during the Third Reich.

Emily's delivery was followed first by silence, then applause, and finally by questions. Lots of questions. Many of the historians present had only heard or read snatches of information about the role of music in concentration camps. They were eager to learn more.

Emily answered questions about the general conditions of the camps, about the unbelievable strength and courage needed for survival alone—not to mention for composing music—and about the various roles music played in the camps.

A few concentration camps had had their own orchestras, and prisoners with musical ability were sometimes able to delay or even escape death by participating in them. Emily explained that even though the prisoners were playing music, this wasn't necessarily a pleasant task for them. Often a group of musicians was forced to accompany prisoners on their way to a grueling fourteen-hour workday in the field or hauling stones—and again as prisoners returned to camp totally exhausted. Sometimes the musicians even had to play for sixteen hours straight.

The musicians were also put into the compromising position of disciplining their fellow prisoners at times. The psychological result was sometimes a feeling of resentment from the other inmates toward the musicians. Because they were not always forced to march themselves, the musicians were sometimes seen as conspirators with the guards or the SS or as the inhumane idiosyncrasies of the Nazis.

As the questions continued, Emily spoke more about the many facets of music in the camps. Music played a role in most concentration camps, and for the SS it was often used as a means of punishment and ironic torture. Musicians were forced to march prisoners to their deaths, for example, or were forced to play for inmates before they were sent to the gas chambers or as they were marched to the trains waiting to transport them from transit camps, like Terezin, to the death camps, like

Auschwitz. Inmates knew what it meant when the orchestra showed up to play for them, and they often reacted to a performance with fear or resignation.

The conference lasted until Sunday morning. When Emily arrived back in Madison around three, Brian was waiting with flowers and a smile. He pulled her close and whispered something in her ear.

Emily kissed Brian warmly and stroked the back of his head. She really had to quit taking him for granted.

Monday morning Emily made her way to the music library and located the information desk. For the first time since the late-night phone call, she began thinking about Hansen's motives for wanting to talk to her. She introduced herself to the librarian and asked to speak with Harold Hansen.

The librarian didn't look up from her newspaper. "He isn't here yet." She looked at her watch and then at Emily. "Hmm, strange, really, because he's never been late before. I wonder if he overslept. Do you want to try back in a bit? In the meantime, I'll let him know you were here when I see him."

Emily thanked the woman and went back to her own office. She had fallen behind with the Chicago conference and needed to get back on track, so she decided to spend the day catching up on paperwork and e-mails and sorting through a large stack of student essays on twentieth-century music.

She started reading the first essay. "Many great musical minds have composed in the twentieth century." Emily groaned and made a note to add a writing unit to the following semester's class.

A knock on the door jolted Emily out of her thoughts. "Come in," she said eagerly, happy to have a reason to put off correcting papers.

The door opened, and her colleague Mark poked his head around the corner. "Is it safe to come in? I imagine you're trying to get caught up after the big conference, but I need to ask your advice about something."

Emily laughed. "Come in, come in. I'm actually happy to have a reason to procrastinate for a minute. We really need to think about incorporating some writing classes into our curriculum. The students have pretty good ideas, but somehow they don't seem able to translate those ideas into meaningful writing."

Emily noticed Mark hadn't moved, and she put down her pen and motioned to a chair for him to take a seat. "What is it you wanted to talk to me about?"

Mark took a seat across from Emily's desk and leaned toward her. "Well, I have a little problem—actually I just need some advice."

Emily ran her fingers through her hair and laughed. She couldn't resist teasing him. "How intriguing. Love trouble again?"

"Ha. Ha. Very funny. You know I've been with the same guy now for almost a year. I think we are soul mates." He batted his lashes at Emily like a love-struck Hollywood actress from the '50s.

Emily rolled her eyes and groaned. "Oh, please, Mark. If you're using that expression *and* batting your eyes, something's off. Besides that, it's one of my most hated phrases—for personal reasons. Now tell me what you need before I kick you out of my office."

Mark's voice took a more serious tone. "You know I've been a member of the musical auditorium board for three years now. Anyway, we've had some trouble recently making ends meet, and we're now looking for ways to boost our ticket sales. To make a long story short, I made the suggestion that we bring some fresh blood into things and spice up our programming a bit. The board liked the idea and of course immediately put me in charge. Now I'm faced with the task of finding innovative, crowd-pleasing composers, musicians, and performers."

Emily laughed and shook her index finger at Mark. "That's what you get for having a great idea!"

He said, "I know, right? Part of me thinks I should have kept my big mouth shut because I've got practically no free time this semester, but a bigger part of me is actually excited by this new challenge. Besides, I need to start padding my dossier for my tenure review in two years. I've started a list of possible candidates, and I was wondering if you wouldn't mind taking a look. I'd love to know your thoughts."

Emily knew that Mark had struggled with getting articles published in highly respected journals, and his teaching record had been marred by a handful of lousy student reviews when he had struggled with serious health problems but had been forced to continue teaching a full load of classes. At this rate it would be difficult for him to fulfill all the requirements for teaching, publishing, and professional service needed for tenure consideration. Emily didn't want to see her one true friend in the department forced to leave. "No problem, Mark. I'd be happy to help. Just let me know when your list is ready." She stood up and waited for him to leave her to her papers.

Instead of taking Emily's obvious cue, Mark leaned back in his chair and pulled a piece of paper out of his jacket pocket. "Actually, I have the finished list right here." He handed the single sheet of paper to Emily. "Would you mind terribly?"

She really needed to get back to grading student essays but felt pinned in a corner. She cast a furtive glance toward the essays and then reached out a hand to take the list. Mark had played his cards perfectly.

Emily quickly scanned the names. She was only vaguely familiar with the first five on the list and quit reading. "Really, Mark?" She handed the paper back to him. "What makes you think these names would draw crowds? Who even knows these people?"

His face looked pained, and Emily quickly regretted her blunt reply. She could be so thoughtless. "Sorry, Mark. I don't mean to sound rude, but I'm wondering how a couple of unknown jazz musicians are going to pull in the crowds we usually get for classical concerts. The auditorium is really known for classical concerts, right? Or are you aiming for a new image?"

He scratched his head. "Actually, no, we're not looking for a new image, but we have a pretty meager budget this year, and I was hoping we could balance some of the more expensive bookings with a few lesser known, but equally talented, individuals." His voice got quiet. "But maybe you're right. Maybe we should just adopt the all-or-nuttin' attitude."

Emily felt her heart clench. His dejection was palpable. "Let me have another look at that list. Your logic is certainly reasonable." As she reexamined the list, her eyes suddenly stopped at a familiar name. Henry Cramer. She looked up at Mark.

"What do you know about this Cramer person?" She set the paper down on the desk. "I heard the most remarkable piece by him just the other night. He might be interesting for us. Provided he's willing to play and lecture here, we could have the local radio play his newest work for a couple of weeks before his visit and then announce that he is lecturing and performing at the auditorium."

Mark moved to the edge of his seat, noticeably more animated than a few seconds before. "I was really hoping you'd choose Cramer, but I didn't want you to say what you thought I wanted to hear. He was my top choice, but I wanted to get another opinion. I actually already called him last week to see if he might be available for a visit. He said he could be here in three weeks. It was the only time he was free for the next several months—and I'd like him to come while we're still able to afford him. I have a feeling he'll be out of our price range by next year. And he's well known enough now with his new piano piece that I think we'll get a good-sized classical crowd on such short notice."

Emily stared at him. "You should think about a career in politics with that poker face, Mark." She pushed the list across her desk toward him. "Sometimes I wonder why I put up with you! Now get out of here. I have essays to grade!"

Later that afternoon, Emily called the library again to ask for Harold Hansen. A woman answered. "Hello again, Ms. Thurgood. We spoke this morning. I'm so sorry, but Mr. Hansen never came in this morning. He didn't call in sick either, and no one has been able to reach him by phone. Would you care to leave a message in case he shows up sometime later today?"

Emily hesitated. She really was eager to find out what Hansen had to show her. "Uh … No, thank you. Maybe I'll just go to his house myself when I'm done here and speak to him there. Could you possibly share his address with me? I noticed he is not in the university directory."

The woman paused before answering. "Well, technically we're not allowed to do that, but …" She hesitated. "I've seen you around the library so much and know who you are. I guess it couldn't hurt. Could you wait a moment please?"

A sharp click followed, and Emily was put on hold. Moments later the woman returned with Hansen's address. "Hello? Are you still there? I have the address for you. It's 12945 Ridgeway Drive. That's on the west side of town. Are you familiar with it? It's not far from the mall."

"I can easily find it on my GPS," Emily quickly replied. "Thank you so very much for your help. Have a great day."

Emily packed up the student essays on her desk, grabbed her coat, and flicked off the light. She knew in her heart that she should finish grading before leaving her office, but she couldn't resist a trip to Hansen's house beforehand.

It was frigid outside, and although Emily turned the car heater on high, the warmth was slow in coming. Someday she'd really have to get that thing fixed. Or get a new car. But on her assistant professor salary she'd have to make do with terminally ill transportation. One week it was the transmission and then the struts—and lots of other things Emily had never even known existed. With her new vocabulary and automotive knowledge, she often mused she could probably gradually work as a mechanic herself someday.

Hansen's house was easy to find, and Emily pulled into the driveway, turned off the car, and got out. As she walked toward the door, her heart suddenly skipped a bit, and she had a slight sinking sensation in her stomach. Her nerves must be playing tricks on her.

She rang the doorbell decisively, hoping the action would push anxiety out of her mind. No one answered, and her palms began to sweat. She rang the bell again and found herself cupping her hands over the sides of her eyes to peer through the window. She couldn't see any movement. When she knocked on the door, it popped open. Emily leaned over the threshold and quietly called out, "Hansen? Harold Hansen? Are you there?" She waited, but there was no response.

She pushed the door open and slowly walked into Hansen's house, immediately catching sight of his large antique book collection. She inspected the titles and saw an extensive array of German authors. She pulled one off the shelf to take a look. Then she spotted her own book *The Will to Compose*. Could that be what Hansen had wanted to talk about? Had something in her book caught his interest? As she fingered the bindings of the books, she remembered that she was in Hansen's house uninvited. She put the book back on the shelf and quickly made her way to the car.

Emily called Hansen when she got home and left a message asking him to call her when he returned. Something didn't feel right about this situation, but she would just have to wait until Hansen contacted her to find out what it was.

Emily spent the rest of the evening correcting student essays. She was happy to note that she had clearly underestimated her students; many of them were beginning to show keen observational skills, and their writing wasn't half bad. She was just finishing the last essay when Brian let himself into her apartment.

"Hey, there, Emily! I brought a friend." Brian held up a bottle of red wine. "I'll fetch the glasses and meet you in the living room."

Emily held up the last essay and waved it at Brian. "Perfect timing! I just finished my last essay."

In typical Emily style, she then headed to the living room and switched on the television without first giving Brian a kiss. She hadn't heard the news in days and wanted to get a quick update. "I hope you don't mind if I watch a summary of the news," she said. "I feel like I have been living in a bubble these past few days."

Brian bent down and gave her a kiss on the lips as he handed her a glass of wine. "I understand, sweetie." He sat down on the couch next to her and watched as the news reporter announced the top stories.

"A new technology high school opened today in Madison. Present were the mayor and several excited parents. The university football team won its fourth game this season, and perhaps most distressing today, a university librarian was found dead in his apartment early this evening. Police are suspecting foul play. After a short commercial break, we will continue with more details on these and other top stories of the day."

Emily stared blankly at the screen. The sinking feeling she'd had on Hansen's doorstep was back. "Oh my God, Brian. Could they be talking about Hansen? I was just at his house a couple of hours ago."

Brian gave Emily a strange look. "Why do you think it could be him? And why on earth were you at his house?"

"Remember how he wanted to meet with me today at the university? Well, he never showed up, and I finally decided to go to his house to see him. And now he might be dead." She ran her hands through her hair and started tapping her foot nervously.

Brian took Emily's hands into his own. "Hold on a sec, Emily. You don't know that or anything else for that matter yet. Let's just watch the rest of the news and find out."

But it was Hansen. They had found him around six o'clock—just one hour after Emily had left his apartment. Someone had apparently made an anonymous call to the police informing them, and they had investigated the call immediately. At the moment the police had no leads and were asking anyone with any information to phone the police.

Emily felt sick. "Brian, I was there. I was in his house." She felt panic rising in her throat. "Oh my God. Maybe Hansen was there the entire time. Do you think he was dead when I was thumbing through his books? Or even worse—was he still alive? Could I have saved him?"

* * *

Seven

News of Hansen's death filled the papers the next day, and the entire music department was buzzing. Actually the entire city was percolating: the grocery store, the laundromat, the bank—unexplained death took a ten on the Richter scale of current events in this small town. The last suspicious death had been fifteen years before. After a two-month disappearance, a French woman's body had been found in Lake Mendota. Rumors had spread quickly that the woman had been killed, but the police had found enough evidence to deem the whole affair a suicide. Eventually the city had moved on.

Hansen's autopsy would take several weeks, and the police were still hunting for clues. The air began to fill with rumors once more. Everyone wondered if Hansen had been killed.

Emily walked around in a state of confusion and felt permanently sick to her stomach. She wondered if she should call the police but doubted she had anything of substance to offer them. After all, Hansen had called her, right? He hadn't told her anything, and she was still in the dark about what he had wanted to tell her. Emily was personally convinced that Hansen had been murdered. He had been so mysterious and anxious on the telephone—and so eager to discuss something with her. Maybe Hansen had even realized he was in danger.

Brian called Emily several times on Tuesday to check on her. He seemed nearly as edgy as Emily about the whole affair and told her he had mixed feelings about whether or not she should get involved.

"Em, I just don't know. Part of me thinks it is a good idea to stay aboveboard on this thing. Maybe you should just call the police, tell them you had some contact with Hansen and were supposed to meet him, and then tell them you were in his apartment the day he was found."

Emily shook her head. "No way, Brian. Do you think I have 'crazy' written across my forehead? If I so much as mention that I was in his apartment that day, I am sure they will arrest me and throw away the key. And what would that do for my tenure review?"

"Um … I think you might be overreacting a bit, don't you think? Isn't it better to be honest and open? It's not like you have anything to hide … um … right?"

Emily snapped, "What do mean 'it's not like I have anything to hide'? Are you doubting me, Brian? Do you seriously think I may have had something to do with this?"

"No, no, of course not. I just think if you withhold any information, the police might decide you're trying to hide something."

Emily bit her lip. "I'm sorry. I guess I'm a little edgy. Maybe you're right. Maybe I *should* tell them about the phone call and the proposed meeting. But there's no way I am telling them about my visit to Hansen's house. It's just too risky."

An hour passed before Emily had summoned the courage to call the police. And when she finally did so, her palms began to sweat, and her thoughts started playing ping-pong. What if they thought she was hiding something? But why should she be afraid of telling the simple truth? She had only wanted to keep an appointment with Hansen. But wasn't that precisely the problem? She hadn't only tried to keep the appointment; she had actually gone into Hansen's house. She thought about how that might be interpreted by the police.

Emily put down the receiver. She needed a pastrami on rye.

She sat in the deli and tried to sort out her thoughts. Maybe she could do some of her own investigating before going to the police to try to come up with some answers. Hansen had wanted to talk to her about something important; theoretically, she should be able to deduce what that thing was.

In the end, not even the sandwich could help her. It was no use. She realized she would have to go to the police. Maybe her contribution would even help the police find some answers. She finished her sandwich, paid, and headed for the door. But before she could leave, she was stopped by a young policeman.

"Ms. Thurgood? Um, are you Ms. Thurgood?" asked the officer tentatively.

Emily felt a prickle on the back of her neck. "Uh, yes, I am Emily Thurgood. Can I help you with something?"

"Someone told us we might find you here. I'm Officer Brisbane. Could you spare a few minutes? We'd like to ask you a few questions."

Emily bit her tongue before she could ask who "someone" was and who "we" referred to and why "they" were looking for her. She forced herself to smile and look the officer in the eye. "I'd be happy to speak with you, Officer. How can I help?"

The officer's cheeks went red. "Um, Ms. Thurgood, could we go to your office or back to the station? I'd rather not conduct this interview in public."

Emily turned and looked around the restaurant. All eyes were on them.

At the police station, the first question came like a blast of cold air: "Ms. Thurgood, we're investigating the death of Harold Hansen. I'm sure you've heard about his death on the news." Brisbane didn't wait for Emily's reply before continuing. "Did you happen to know Mr. Hansen personally?"

Emily found herself hesitating. "Uh, only vaguely. I met him at a party about four months ago."

Brisbane jotted something down in a small notebook. "I see. So you hadn't seen Mr. Hansen since that party, is that correct?"

"Yes, that's right." Emily was relieved she didn't have to lie at all. Technically she hadn't "seen" Hansen at all since that party.

"So you haven't had any contact with him at all since then?"

Emily's palms began to sweat. Now they were entering gray territory. "Actually, Hansen called me on the phone about a week or so ago."

The officer leaned closer to Emily and almost whispered his next question. "Really? Why was that? What did you talk about with Hansen?"

Why was he talking so softly? Did that mean he knew about the call already? Emily wiped her palms off on her pants. "We didn't talk long. He wanted to meet with me, but I was in the middle of preparing for a conference presentation and had no time. We made arrangements to meet yesterday—Monday, the day he was found."

"That explains the calendar entry we found on his desk." The officer made some more notes. "Tell me what happened at the meeting. You did keep the appointment, correct?"

Emily found herself telling Brisbane everything—apart from the unorthodox tour of Hansen's house. From what she could tell, the officer appeared satisfied, thanked her for her time, and asked her to stay in town in case they had more questions.

Emily agreed and asked one final question. "By the way, have the police decided if it was a suicide or not?" (She wasn't prepared to voice the alternative.)

The officer stood and held out his hand to Emily. "Thanks for your time. Actually, they've decided it was indeed a case of foul play. The autopsy will take some time, but they already found a fair amount of Paris green in Hansen's blood—are you familiar with that substance? It's generally used to kill weeds."

Emily was extremely familiar with it—she used it every year in her garden. She decided to keep that information to herself for the time being. "What a horrible way to die!"

"Any way to die is a horrible way to die," said Brisbane as he saw Emily to the door.

* * *

EIGHT

The next day was relatively calm. Apart from a few meetings, Emily was left with an abundance of free time to think about Hansen and what had happened. She was sure she was forgetting something that she and Hansen had talked about at the party. They had talked about her book and a recipe for Swedish meatballs, but that was all Emily could remember. And Hansen wouldn't have needed to contact her in the middle of the night for a meatball recipe. Was it something in her book after all?

A knock on her office door made her jump. It was Hansen's ex-wife, Gloria, whom Emily had recently met for the first time that morning at the memorial service.

"Professor Thurgood? Excuse me, do you have a moment?"

Emily felt a strange tightening in her throat and invited her to come in. "Please call me Emily. Have a seat. Can I get you some tea? Or some coffee perhaps?"

Gloria fiddled with the handle of her purse as she took a seat. "No, thank you very much, but there is something I'd like to ask you about if you don't mind."

"Anything."

"Well, I just came to Madison for the service. Harold and I haven't—uh, hadn't—really seen much of each other these past few years, but I did consider him to be my friend, and we did talk on the phone regularly." She tightened her hold on her bag. "Anyway, the police pulled me aside after the service—can you imagine the timing?—and asked me all kinds of weird personal questions about my marriage to Harold, why we got divorced, what our relationship was like when we were married, if we ever fought seriously—things like that. Maybe it was my imagination, but they seemed to be hinting that I had something to do with Harold's death. They even asked me to volunteer fingerprints."

Emily nodded. She wasn't sure why Hansen's ex-wife was confiding in her, but she wanted to wait until Gloria was finished before jumping in.

Gloria seemed to be watching Emily's eyes very closely. "In the course of my conversation with the police—I guess interrogation is a more appropriate word for it—they mentioned your name a couple of times and asked if I knew you."

Emily felt prickles slowly crawling up the back of her neck.

Gloria looked Emily directly in the eye and leaned forward, putting one hand on her desk. "How well did you know my ex-husband, Ms. Thurgood? May I ask what your relationship with him was?"

It was definitely time for Emily to open her mouth. "First of all, please call me Emily. I assume it's okay for me to call you Gloria?"

Gloria nodded, and Emily continued, "Second, I didn't have a relationship with Harold. I only met him once at a party and then had an extremely brief phone conversation with him. I have no idea why the police mentioned my name to you. They did question me as well if that's any consolation. They are probably just trying to cover their bases."

"Maybe …" Gloria paused before continuing. "Emily … I need to know what happened to Harold. Is there something you're not telling the police? Did you have something to do with his murder?"

Emily was stunned. She had barely known the man. Why would she want to kill him? Emily inhaled sharply and said, "I understand your need to find out who murdered your husband … um, sorry—ex-husband. But that doesn't give you the right to come in here and accuse me of killing him. I think I would like you to leave my office now, please." Emily stood up and looked at the door.

Gloria held up a hand. "No, wait. I'm sorry. It's just that …"

"It's just that what, Gloria?"

"It's just that my ex-husband mentioned you to me several times. Well, not you exactly, but your last book. Apparently there was something in it that he really liked or hated or something. I'm sorry I can't remember all the details. I guess I wasn't listening that closely. He often talked about things he had read, and most of it went in one ear and out the other, but I do remember him mentioning you and your book."

Emily smiled. “Well, that hardly seems like a good reason for me to kill him.”

“Maybe not, but the police seemed to be very interested when I told them about my husband’s interest in you—uh, your book.”

Emily would soon find out how very interested the police really were.

* * *

NINE

The next two weeks passed in a blur as Emily threw herself into work and tried not to think about murdered librarians. The composer Henry Cramer was scheduled to hold a master class and perform two concerts on Thursday, and before Emily could refuse, Mark had managed to get her to agree to act as official hostess. As she made a grocery list for the reception at her house that evening, her mind kept wandering back to Hansen. Was it mere coincidence that he had been killed the day she was supposed to meet him? Did his murder have something to do with her after all? If so, what was the connection? The most logical tie between them was her book or music in general, but maybe there was something else she was missing. She decided to have another look at her book after the reception. Maybe there was a clue hiding in the book. Or maybe it was just a coincidence after all that Hansen had been killed on the day he was supposed to meet with her. Who would want to kill a music librarian anyway?

Emily looked down at her list. Olives, wine, tomatoes, suspects, motives? It wouldn't be easy to find the last two items at the grocery store—or anywhere for that matter.

Cramer's first selection was brilliant. As everyone had hoped, he began with his piano sonata. It was even more beautiful than Emily had remembered. The loneliness seemed more pronounced in a live performance, and the striking rhythms more urgent. There was something familiarly haunting about the piece—something Emily couldn't put her finger on.

Compared to the sonata, the rest of the pieces on the program seemed almost like an afterthought. Solid, clear rhythmic lines made the selections interesting, but something was missing—or maybe it was just the lack of contrasts of melody and rhythm.

After the concert was over, it was no surprise to Emily that everyone seemed most intrigued by the sonata. There were many questions about the origins of the piece, its compositional structure, and its relationship to the traditional sonata form.

Cramer seemed remarkably modest to Emily. The sonata was an obvious masterpiece, and he seemed strangely apologetic in his responses. "I didn't spend hours carefully planning the movements and their relationship to each other. And I certainly didn't spend months analyzing how my sonata was going to fit into the historical development of the piano sonata."

The audience laughed. "Frankly," Cramer continued, "this piece wrote itself for the most part."

He seemed almost to prefer talking about his other pieces and drew the audience's attention back to the remainder of his program. "The second work you heard tonight—the *Six Little Pieces*—was a much more difficult birth, for example. Each segment is intricately related—both tonally and rhythmically. The trick was to create something new, something individual." He took a sip of water. "So many composers today sound the same, and I think our greatest challenge as modern artists is to find that unchartered territory. Sometimes it feels as though there's no unchartered musical land left to discover. We are modern-day explorers."

Emily was thrilled when Mark took the opportunity to end the question-answer session. Cramer's Columbus metaphors were more than she could stomach, and besides, she really wanted to learn more about that sonata. She would have to find another time to ask him about it.

The next morning over coffee, Cramer was clearly as fascinated with Emily's work as she was with his sonata. "I've read your most recent book—*The Will to Compose*. I was so thrilled to have a chance to come to your university. It was great of Mark to allow me to speak and play here. I'll confess I've wanted to meet you for quite some time."

Emily was caught off guard. *Allow?* Hadn't Mark been the one to solicit Cramer to come to the university? Surely he had meant *invite*? She made a mental note to talk to Mark later. She smiled at Cramer. "The pleasure is all mine. I'll never forget the first time I heard your sonata. I was sitting in my car, and—"

He interrupted Emily before she could continue. "Please, Ms. Thurgood, let's not talk now about the sonata. Frankly, I'm a little tired of that piece. Do you mind if I ask you some questions about your work instead?"

Emily had so many questions for Cramer, but he was the guest after all. "Please, call me Emily. Of course, you can ask me anything."

"Okay, Emily. Call me Henry then. No more Mr. Cramer."

"Agreed."

"Anyway, I feel so fortunate to be able to talk about your research with you in person. Your work is very original and fundamentally important for the musical community. Of course, I knew that many composers who ended up in concentration camps continued writing music—Messiaen being perhaps the best known of all of them. I almost decided to get some of your music students to perform his *Quartet for the End of Time* with me last night, and then I decided I had better stick to original works."

Emily had to admit she was intrigued. Her research usually appealed to a small, niche audience. She was a bit surprised to find Henry among her admirers.

He took a sip of coffee before continuing. "Anyway, I was familiar with Messiaen but certainly not with many of the other musicians and composers you discuss in your book. Would you mind telling me more about Felix Steinitz?" Henry reached across the table and touched her arm. "Or are you tired of always talking about this topic?"

Emily quickly leaned back against her chair and crossed her arms in front of her. Her arm was tingling where his hand had been. "No, of course not." She smiled. "I am actually usually trying to get people to listen to me. I'd love to talk about Steinitz or anything else from my book for that matter. It's a passion for me." She leaned forward a bit but kept distance between them. "What would you like to know?"

Henry chuckled. "Well, can you start at the beginning? I've got some free time before I have to give the composition master class this afternoon. Maybe we could turn this coffee into lunch. I'd love to know how you discovered Steinitz. I understand finding him really pulled you into this topic in the first place."

Emily wondered how he could know that. That wasn't in her book.

Henry must have noticed her furrowed brow, and he explained, "One of my colleagues at the college attended a presentation you gave a couple of years back in San Francisco, and she told me about your interest in this area. I picked her brain about you and your presentation. That was before your book came out, so you can imagine how eager I was to see your work in print."

He had asked about her? The air suddenly seemed thick, and Emily coughed slightly. She wondered if she had remembered to put her inhaler in her purse. She asked him if they could pay and step outside. "Must be my asthma acting up," Emily said.

Once outside, they walked around the university campus. Henry seemed to be standing just a bit too close, but Emily decided it was just her asthma making her feel claustrophobic.

When Henry invited Emily to join him for lunch, she obligingly agreed. After all, she was his designated host for the day. She couldn't exactly abandon him to his own devices. Emily suggested a small French bistro on the west side of campus. They didn't have pastrami on rye sandwiches, but Emily ordered the next best thing instead: a ham-and-broccoli quiche. As they waited for their food to arrive, Cramer asked Emily how she had developed an interest in Steinitz and his work.

"As is often the case with these things, it was really just an accident. One semester, while studying Brecht and Weill's opera *Rise and Fall of the City of Mahagonny*, I stumbled across a short reference to Felix Steinitz. It wasn't anything major—just his name mentioned in the middle of a discussion about another artist. But I looked at the name again to see if I had read it correctly. I had read virtually everything on Brecht and Weill's collaboration and on artists from that period, but I had never even seen Steinitz's name before. I had also never heard him mentioned by anyone in the music community." Emily stopped talking long enough to take a sip of water. She was unnerved to notice Henry's eyes following her movements as she lifted the glass to her lips. "Anyway, my curiosity was piqued, and the usual questions popped into my head. Who was this Felix Steinitz? What role had he played in twentieth-century music? Was he an amateur or a forgotten gifted composer? I was determined from that point onward to find out whatever I could about him."

Henry leaned forward and took Emily's hand. "This is exactly what I expected from you. You are a passionate researcher who looks for pieces to a historical puzzle. I knew I wouldn't be disappointed."

Emily gave his hand a cursory squeeze before pulling her hand back to wipe her mouth with her napkin. She avoided his eyes. "That all sounds much more romantic than it really was. I just really wanted to know more. And you know, Henry, this wouldn't have been the first composer to get lost in the shuffle of the twentieth century. Traditional history is far too selective: isolated names and movements are singled out as significant, while seemingly secondary composers are ignored or forgotten."

Henry hadn't stopped looking at Emily. "So what did you find out?"

"Well, the more I explored libraries and archives, the more I realized just what a remarkable man Steinitz really was. He had been a versatile individual who had worked as a composer, pianist, music critic, conductor, and opera coach."

"That's quite a list of accomplishments for any one person."

"Yes, but the more I researched him, the more I was moved by Steinitz's moral courage above all else. In the middle of his career, in 1942, Steinitz had been deported to the concentration camp Terezin. And despite the sometimes life-threatening restrictions and conditions, he found a way to continue his activities as a composer while in Terezin, even managing to write over twenty compositions in two years. I believe he even managed to escape death by working so actively as a musician and composer. They needed him to keep producing music."

Emily paused as their food arrived and realized she had been the only one talking. She apologized for rambling on.

Henry laughed. "Not at all. This is utterly fascinating for me. Remember—I am also a composer. I personally find it nearly impossible to compose under the best of conditions. Anyone who can compose and work creatively under such extreme circumstances must have been made from tough stuff indeed. Please continue."

Emily took a small bite of her ham-and-broccoli quiche. "Well, what struck me most about all of this were the signs of hope and faith in a fundamentally hopeless situation. Music provided some of the prisoners with a semblance of humanity in a barbaric system that attempted to rob them of their very person. Music allowed them to keep part of their souls intact, to establish some sense of solidarity, to provide a glimmer of light in a very dark world. And at some camps music was an integral part of the culture and was promoted and encouraged by the guards. But at others, musicians often wrote and sang or played at the risk of death."

Henry put down his fork. "Did you ever wonder what drove them to take such risks?"

"Yes, of course. I often wonder why a composer would risk his life to compose in such a situation. And how Steinitz managed to write so much music in his two years at Terezin. And what the conditions were like under which he had written. Think about the simple things that we take for granted, like where he had found the paper? How many other composers were doing the same thing?"

"And were you able to answer all these questions, Emily?"

"Not all of them, no. Steinitz had passed away by the time I discovered him, so I couldn't talk to him directly. But as I dug deeper, I realized that even though Steinitz had died, there might be some survivors who were still alive who I could speak to about him."

Henry reached across the table to touch Emily's arm. "And were you able to find anyone who remembered him?"

Emily was not fond of strangers touching her. She flashed him a quick smile before pulling away to reach for her glass of water. She took a sip before continuing. "I was very lucky to find two men who had been at the concentration camp Terezin with Steinitz, and they were gracious enough to allow me to ask them about that very distressing time. I was also able to get my hands on some of Steinitz's scores from that period. The more I worked, the more I became aware that Steinitz had used his music as a source of comfort and hope for the prisoners." Emily put her fork down so she could better use her hands to support her storytelling. "Like many other musicians, he coded his criticism in sanctioned language and music, but the prisoners knew what he was hiding between the lines and could draw strength from his music."

Henry jumped in. "I've heard quite a bit about artists in the same situation who were forced to hide their drawings in the floor or in the walls. They had to be very resourceful to get the simple tools they needed."

"Yes, that's right. For the composers and musicians it was no different. As you said yourself, Messiaen was in a similar predicament. In 1940, while he was held at a German prison camp, he discovered three musicians among his fellow inmates: a clarinetist, a cellist, and a violinist. He had to make do with a violin, a clarinet, and a cello with one string missing for the beginning of his *Quartet for the End of Time*. Those were simply the only instruments around. Later, before he actually even had one, he added a piano to the quartet. Luckily, he was eventually able to find a piano in the camp—granted, it was in terrible shape, but at least it was a piano. These composers and, as you say, the artists as well were remarkably resourceful. The act of writing alone involved finding something to write with and something to write on—both things we entirely take for granted today."

Emily noticed that Henry had finished eating while she had only a single bite of quiche missing from her plate. "I must apologize, Henry." She pointed to her plate. "This always happens when the lunch or dinner conversation turns to my work. I manipulate the entire conversation."

He shook his head and smiled. "That couldn't be further from the truth. I asked you to tell me about your journey in finding Steinitz, and you were merely humoring me."

"You are too kind. Now please tell me something about yourself and your work, so I don't feel so selfish." She picked up her fork and took another bite of her quiche.

Henry wiped his mouth and set his napkin on the table. "I'm afraid I am not as naturally gifted and passionate as you are, Emily. I tend to schedule my composition time for the same time every day and approach it like clockwork."

Emily shook her head. "That's not a bad thing. I know plenty of writers who swear by that method."

"I love music more than anything. But I'll be honest: at the moment everyone seems completely focused on my piano sonata. And like I said at the concert last night, I sometimes do feel that it wrote itself. One of those famous 'inspirational' bursts of energy." He signed quotation marks at the word *inspirational* with his fingers.

Emily was surprised and confused by Henry's response. "Is there anything wrong with that? I believe it's called 'inspiration' for a reason."

Henry shook his head. "Don't get me wrong. I do believe there may have been a higher force guiding me through that piece, but I also wonder if that burst wasn't a one-time thing, as though my fifteen minutes of fame might be limited to that one little piece." He looked down at the tablecloth.

Emily was kicking herself for making him feel uncomfortable. She should have remembered how sensitive musicians could be. "I'm sure you'll write many more pieces like that one, Henry. Anyone who can do it once has the gift to do it again."

Henry looked at his watch. "We should probably finish up here and get back to the university. As you already know, I have a three-hour master class at one o'clock." He once again reached across the table for Emily's hand. "Will I see you again later today?"

Emily avoided looking him in the eye and mumbled something about afternoon meetings and appointments. She promised to pick him up around four after his master class and waved to the waitress to pay for lunch.

* * *

Ten

Back in her office, Emily was unable to concentrate. She couldn't help but wonder about Henry's intentions, the many times he had touched her hand or arm. His questions about her work had also seemed to go beyond a scholarly interest. And had he really specifically asked Mark if he could visit the university, so he could meet her in person?

She picked up the phone and dialed Mark's office number. She needed to ask him more about Cramer's university visit.

"Hey, Mark, this is Emily. I just came from coffee and lunch with Henry—uh, Henry Cramer."

Emily heard Mark cover the receiver with his hand and mumble something to someone in his office. "Hey, Emily. Sorry about that. I just had a visit from the police, but they just left."

"The police?"

"Yeah, I know, right? Pretty weird stuff, but apparently they wanted to know about our relationship—mine and yours."

Emily almost dropped the phone. "Our *what*? We don't have a relationship."

He laughed. "Of course, I am aware of that. Not that kind of relationship, Em. Just—you know—how I know you, how we met, what our connections are at the university. Nothing kinky."

Emily was still confused. "Why would they want to know that?" Emily dropped her voice to a conspiring whisper. "What did you tell them, darling?"

He laughed again. "Very funny, Em. I told them the truth. We work together, we've known each other for a couple of years, and we have a wonderful professional relationship." He paused before continuing.

"Oh, and that I am sure you are involved in systematically murdering off faculty and staff at the university."

"Mark! That's not remotely funny. What did you really say?" Emily's hands suddenly felt moist.

"Nothing. I said nothing. I did ask them why they wanted to know, though."

"Did they tell you?"

He paused. "Yes."

"Mark, don't do this to me. What did they say?"

"They said you might be a person of interest. Now, to what do I owe the pleasure of this call, Emily?"

"A person of interest?" Emily's palms were now hot. She shook her head to clear it and said, "It seems silly compared to what you just shared with me, but I was wondering about Cramer. He told me he approached you and asked if he could visit our university. He said he was a big fan of mine and was thrilled to be able to meet me. I'm just wondering why you told me that it was your idea to invite him here? Why didn't you tell me that he approached you?"

The silence was deafening. "Mark, are you still there?"

"Emily, I made it all up."

Emily was confused. "Made what up?"

"Everything. The list, the pressure to find musicians and performers—all of it."

"But why?"

"If I tell you, will you promise to keep it to yourself?"

"Yes."

"I'm embarrassed to say this, but I really needed the money."

Emily didn't understand. "What money? Who gave you money?"

"He did."

"Who?"

"Cramer. He gave me a lot of money to invite him here, so he could meet you. He asked me to keep it a secret. He didn't want anyone to know—especially not you. Emily? Please don't think less of me. I am in danger of foreclosing on my house, and I really needed the money."

The room seemed to close in on Emily, and she grasped the phone tightly with both hands. "I don't know what to say. Why would he do this? He could have called me personally or asked to speak with me directly."

"I really don't know. I swore to him I wouldn't tell you any of this, but it's honestly getting a little weird. I have a feeling he wanted you to think his visit to the university was purely professional."

* * *

Emily didn't know how she could face Cramer after his master class, but she had agreed to be his designated host for the entire day. She wondered if he had paid Mark extra for that as well. As she slowly walked to the studio, she mulled over what Mark had just told her. Why had Cramer gone to such great lengths to meet her under false pretenses? He could just as easily have called her on the phone or e-mailed her.

Cramer looked flushed when he came out of the studio.

"Everything all right? You look a little worn out."

Henry wiped his brow and laughed. "Yes, well, your students worked me hard. I think I'm ready for a drink. Are you game?"

After her phone call with Mark and Cramer's own overly friendly demeanor earlier that day, Emily was wishing she could bow out of having cocktails with him, but she didn't wish to be rude. "Of course. What did you have in mind?"

Cramer took Emily by the arm and escorted her to the door. "Why don't you surprise me? Something more intimate perhaps?"

More intimate? It was time to set the record straight. "Uh, Mr. Cramer …"

"Henry."

"Uh, Henry, you need to know that I am seeing someone."

Cramer stopped walking to look Emily in the eye. "And why do I need to know that?"

His direct manner was quite unnerving. Emily felt a flutter in her chest. "Well, I thought …"

"You thought that I was hitting on you?"

"Well, in a manner of speaking—yes."

Cramer tilted his head back and laughed. "If I didn't have a girlfriend back in Toledo, I might be the first in line for that job, Emily. You are extremely attractive, talented, and bright. Who wouldn't want to hit on you?"

Somehow his denial wasn't convincing her, but she decided to take him at his word. "I'm sorry. I just thought ..."

"No worries. Now, where would you like to lead me?" He bowed in her direction and made a sweeping gesture with his arm.

Over drinks, the talk returned to Emily's work. Each time she tried to steer the conversation back to Henry's compositions, he managed to connect something back to Emily's research. "Speaking of composition, I'd love to know how you went from discovering Steinitz to practically devoting the next three years to finding other musicians and composers who had also been in concentration camps."

Emily took a sip of Chardonnay and told Henry about her research. Talking about her work was familiar ground and put her at ease. "It was very easy really. Earlier today, I told you that I talked to some survivors about Steinitz. Well, once I had established a personal connection to some of them, it was like being pulled into this great big extended family. The first survivors I spoke with introduced me to other people who had already interviewed them, and they then led me to other individuals whose main goal was to look for answers to one of the most puzzling and gruesome periods in history."

Henry popped a handful of nuts in his mouth. "I'm sure you also visited some archives."

Emily nodded. "Yes, in Prague I did a lot of work in archives—I even managed to find some pretty big personal family archives. Some families even opened up their homes and hearts to me completely. One woman's brother had also been at Terezin, and a lot of his music had miraculously made it back to her. She and her husband had immigrated to the States during the war. I'm still not sure how her brother's music was saved from destruction, but much of it was recovered." Emily looked at Henry to see if she should continue.

"Please go on."

"Anyway, this woman, Gabi, moved back to Germany with her husband and kids when the war was over. Isn't that incredible? Can you imagine moving back to a country that had tried to wipe out everyone who was like you?"

Henry shook his head. "Never."

"Well, Gabi's native language was German, and Germany was her home country. They never really felt comfortable in the United States and wanted to go back."

Henry waved to the waitress for another round of drinks. Emily held up a hand. "Oh, uh, I should probably limit myself. I still have quite a bit of work to do."

"The day is young. You can have a couple of drinks and still get some work done later. Besides, you still haven't told me if you found any women composers from that time."

Emily was impressed that Henry had noticed all her composers had been men. "Interesting question, Henry. You know yourself that female composers aren't nearly as recognized as male composers historically. At least there haven't been that many over the years. Of course, there are some well-known exceptions, most notably, the likes of Clara Schumann and Fanny Mendelssohn, but even those shared the limelight with their more famous male relatives. Now imagine the situation in the concentration camps—there weren't even that many men composing. It was simply too dangerous."

"But surely there were some female musicians held in the camps? Did any of them play at that time?"

The waitress returned with their drinks, and Emily nodded. "Yes, I did hear about a woman's orchestra in Dachau. They also had a female conductor, but as far as I can tell, there weren't any female composers—at least at that camp. Of course there may have been several women composing at the camps, but it's really difficult—almost impossible, really, to say exactly what was going on."

Emily stopped to look at Henry. "Why are you so interested?"

Henry's hand brushed Emily's as he reached for a napkin, and Emily felt a brief jolt of electricity. "No reason, really. My mother composed a bit; that's all. And as I told you before, I'm always curious about the conditions under which people were able to compose."

Emily took the opportunity to change the subject back to Henry. "Enough about me and my work. I know you're tired of people asking you about it, but humor me and tell me about your piano sonata. How did you start the piece, where did you get your ideas, and how long did it take you to write it? I'm always fascinated by how long it takes people to write things. Morbid fascination, I guess."

"Well, it didn't take long to write at all. Maybe a month—maybe less. You know I've heard of writers participating in marathon novel writing sessions every November. They call it NaNoWriMo—National Novel Writing Month. I can't begin to imagine writing a complete novel in such a short period of time, but I guess I did something similar with my sonata."

Emily had heard about those marathon writing sessions and had been tempted herself to try to write a novel. Maybe after her next music history book. She asked Henry for more information about his piece. "How did you get your ideas for the sonata?"

Henry was tapping a rhythm on the table with his right index finger. Emily tried to guess the piece as Henry said, "That's a tough question. I guess I've been influenced by the Second Viennese School. I know it's really outdated by today's standards, but I'm quite fascinated by the twelve-tone scale—I didn't follow the compositional rules for the sonata form very rigidly, but then again, I don't have Schoenberg breathing down my neck either, do I?"

The wine was making Emily relax, and she laughed warmly. "Good choice to find a mentor who's no longer around to pick on you! Let's toast to that."

Henry smiled and lifted his glass. "I like the way you think, Emily!"

The next morning, Emily had some difficulty piecing together what had happened next. She remembered their conversation about composers and composition and could definitely remember a couple of glasses of Chardonnay, but after that, things got fuzzy. Had they really had so much to drink? It wasn't like her to have more than two drinks, especially with a professional contact. But her head was pounding, and she felt a burning thirst. She needed water and then a strong cup of coffee.

Why couldn't she remember what had happened? She also still remained convinced that Henry was attracted to her. Surely things hadn't gotten physical?

The phone rang, drawing Emily out of her thoughts. "Ms. Thurgood?"

Emily held a hand to her head. "Yes, speaking. Who is this?"

"That's not important right now. I understand you're involved in a murder."

Emily inhaled sharply. "Who is this, and what do you want from me?"

The voice was so muffled she couldn't tell if it was a man or a woman speaking. "That is unimportant right now. I know you didn't kill anyone, but there are people who believe you did. I am calling to give you some free advice."

Emily's knuckles turned white as she grasped the receiver more tightly. "Who is this? What do you know about Hansen's death?"

"My identity is unimportant at the moment. I left you something at your office. Take it seriously."

"What is it?"

"I just have one piece of advice for you. If you want to exonerate yourself, look to the music."

Emily heard a click. "Wait! Wait! What does that mean? Exonerate myself? For what? What music? Who is this?" The only answer Emily got was a dial tone.

While her coffee brewed, Emily took a hot shower and got ready for work. She wanted to get to work early to see what the mysterious person had left for her and what the cryptic message might mean. She also had a class at nine o'clock and needed to focus. She worked on washing away her headache with the hot water, but it was only replaced with a sense of dread. It was becoming clear that she was in trouble. She just wondered how much trouble.

When she arrived at her office, Emily scanned the room to see if anything was out of place. Her desk was exactly as she had left it: a pile of disorganized papers, Post-it notes, and a crumpled sandwich wrapper from the Village Deli. Her bookshelves also appeared to be untouched. She emptied the dirty ashtray on her desk and moved some papers around. Nothing seemed to be out of the ordinary. She walked down the hallway to the department secretary to ask if anyone had left anything for her while she was gone. Nothing. Was this some kind of joke?

Emily shook it off and decided to focus on her next class. She had to stay one step ahead of her students and was feeling anything but prepared for the lively discussion they were sure to give her. Her thoughts kept wandering to Hansen and what he might have wanted to show her. And to the mysterious voice and what might have been left for her and where it might be hiding in her office.

Mark poked his head around her door. "Hey, Emily, I can't thank you enough. I just got back from driving Cramer to the airport. He talked about you the entire way there. If I didn't know better, I'd think he'd fallen …" He stopped talking to look at Emily. "Are you okay? You look like you've seen a ghost. Are you feeling all right?"

"I'm fine. There's a lot going on right now, and things seem to get stranger every day. Plus I was so busy entertaining Cramer that I had temporarily forgotten about the whole murdered librarian thing. I had a sobering reminder about that this morning. And speaking of sobering, I have an awful hangover and unfortunately need to go teach in a few minutes."

Mark walked into her office and took a seat. "What happened this morning?"

"Some mysterious person called me at home claiming to know who the real killer is."

"What? You should go to the police."

"And tell them what? That I should 'look to the music'?"

"Look to the music? What does that mean?"

Emily ran her hands through her hair. "You tell me. I'm about ready to lose it, Mark. This person who called me also claimed to have left something for me in my office, but there's nothing here—at least as far as I can tell."

Mark motioned to the papers on Emily's desk. "Well, it's not like your desk is exactly organized, Emily. Maybe there's something buried in all that junk."

"I guess that's possible, but I don't have time right now to sort through all this stuff. I've been frantically busy lately and am way behind schedule with my class prep. I worked like a maniac to get ready for the conference, then some virtual stranger I was supposed to meet was murdered, and then we had a more than mildly flirtatious guest I had to host for an entire day. I am frazzled to say the least."

* * *

Eleven

July 1943

Anna needed to find a way to stay sane. If she couldn't escape Terezin, then she would have to create an alternative world, one in which she and the others could hold the psychological upper hand and the power to prevail. She brought the women together in a group for their daily practice session and whispered to them her plan. Each night, as they rehearsed the text and music of Verdi's Requiem, Anna would quietly and secretly write her own music.

Anna had to plan carefully. Paper was a rare commodity, but if she took only single sheets at a time from the main music room, she was fairly sure she wouldn't be caught. She would need to find a way to smuggle the pages out one by one. That would be difficult, but perhaps Steinitz or Schächter could help her?

She started by choosing a familiar German Workers' Movement chant from the 1920s to inspire herself and the other prisoners at Terezin. She chose German because it was the common language for all nationalities at the camp; this chant had also been used by the proletariat in its fight to survive. *Gebt den Glauben nicht Auf. Die Freiheit siegt! Wir werden befreit!* Don't stop believing. Freedom will prevail! We will be freed!

She would have to mask the revolutionary words of the chant somehow but keep their essence so the piece she was writing could hold a message. How would she do that? Anna tapped the pencil on the table.

Anna decided to start with the melody from the German folk song "Marschieren im Wald" ("Marching in the Forest") and used it as the primary melody. The uninitiated listener would assume that was the main piece she was setting words to. She set that melody down on paper and contemplated her next move. She looked at the chant and played with different musical ideas to mask the revolutionary message. The first letter of each word? Would that work?

Gebt den Glauben nicht auf ... *G, G, N, A* ... *G* was easy. She could use the key of G for the basis, but what would she do with *N*?

Anna jotted down "key of G, key of A."

Die Freiheit siegt ... *D, F* ...

Key of D, F ... How would she handle *S*?

Wir werden befreit ... *W, W, B* ... The key of B would fit in nicely, but what about *W*?

Anna bit the end of her pencil. What would she do with *N*, *S*, and *W*?

From the window, she saw a guard approaching the door. She quickly stuffed the piece of paper into her shirt and motioned to the women to gather around to sing Verdi.

As she sang the Latin lines of Verdi's piece, Anna thought about letters, notes, and keys. How could she bring them all together in musical form?

A guard patrolling outside stopped to listen to the women rehearse, and then he moved on to check on the men in another building. Anna quickly pulled out her sheet of paper and started writing notes to herself before she forgot what she wanted to write next.

As a child Anna had learned Russian and German in addition to her native Czech, and she now had an idea. The names of the musical keys from the Cyrillic and German alphabets could help her. She wrote down the letter *N* from the word *nicht*. She couldn't give up this important word in her coded musical piece. Do *not* give up. The message was central to their fight. She wrote down the Cyrillic representation for *N*, which was written as *H*. *Perfect,* she thought to herself and then took it one step further. If she converted that *H* from Cyrillic to the German musical system, she would end up with the key of B because, as she had learned at the conservatory, *H* was the representation for the key of B in German. Similarly, she could take the initial *V* sound from the German letter *W* from the words *Wir* and *werden* in the poem and again replace it with the Cyrillic equivalent, which was *B*. In German *B* was the key of B-flat. She wrote down "B flat."

Anna looked at her notes and smiled. The mental challenge made her happy. All letters were accounted for except *S*. How could she represent it musically? She stared out the window and reviewed what she could remember from the German musical key system. She struggled to remember, and then it occurred to her that *S* was the key of E-flat in German.

The importance of using Cyrillic and German in her coded musical message did not escape Anna. The hope for Russian liberation from the German camp was increasingly talked about in hushed tones. Hiding this hope in music would allow them to sing their hope out loud.

Anna took the important letters and musical keys and used them for the counter melody in the musical piece. She drew a line across the paper and lined up the notes for the letters of the chant underneath it. G, G, B, A, D, F, E-flat, B-flat, B-flat, B-flat … Anna tapped the pencil on the paper and closed her eyes, imagining the white and black keys of the piano. In Prague she had done all her composing at the piano. Here she would have to imagine the keyboard in her mind's eye. The keys floated in front of her now. She could see the key of G: G, B, D. If she added an F, she could hear a minor ninth chord in the key of G. She opened her eyes and looked at the paper. What letters were left? A, E-flat, and B-flat floated off the page. Key of E-flat? She visualized the notes E-flat, G, and B-flat.

The door burst open, and a guard entered the room. Anna had just enough time to stash the paper and pencil before he rushed over to where she was sitting with the other women. He pointed to Lexa and three other women next to her. "You four. Pack your bags and go to the train. *Now.* You are being moved to the east." The guard turned his rifle toward the rest of the women. "And *you* women. You will accompany those girls in song as they march onto their train."

The guards ordered the singers to line up along the path to the train. A drummer and clarinetist had been located as well, and the group was told to sing and play the traditional Yiddish camp song "Arum dem Fayer" ("Around the Fire"). The musicians started the first notes of the song, and the guard told them to stop. "Livelier! Livelier! This is happy music. It is a happy trip your friends are taking!"

The musicians started again and played faster. The opening bars of the song were clarinet and drum only, and the drummer set the beat. The clarinetist joined in—at first slowly and then much livelier as the guard again ordered him to pick up the pace. The singers then joined in. As they sang the lyrics, Anna tasted salt and felt her throat grow thick. She forced the bile back down and forced herself to sing what she knew was never again to be an innocent song of singing by the fire.

Arum dem fayer
Mir zingen lider
Di nakht iz tayer men vert nit midn
Un zol der fayer far loshn vern
Shoynt oyf der himl mir zaynen shtern

To kroynt di kop mit blumen krantsn
Arum dem fayer mir freylekh tantsn
Vayl tants un lid iz undzer lebn
Der nokh in shlof khaloymes shvebn

Around the fire
We're singing songs
The night is special, and we are not tired
And as the fire burns down to ashes
The heavens shine on us with starlight

We wrap our heads with flowering crowns
Around the fire we're dancing happily
To dance to music is our life
And in our sleep our dreams come calling

Anna tried not to think about where the trains were going. There would be fire and ashes, but she knew no one would be dancing happily. She knew in her heart that she would never see her beloved friends again.

* * *

TWELVE

January 2014

Emily hadn't had a chance to talk to Brian, but when she got home, she found several messages from him on her home answering machine. The last one sounded particularly energetic. "Emily, where are you? I've been trying to reach you for hours. Please call me. I think I can help you with your little problem."

She called him immediately. "What problem, Brian?"

"Hello to you too! I am fine. How have you been?"

Emily ran her fingers through her hair and breathed in deeply. "Sorry. It's been a rough couple of days, and I just now got all of your messages. What little problem were you talking about?"

Brian's voice was low. "Well, it's no secret that the police have visited several people about you. They seem to believe you are a prime suspect in that librarian's death."

Emily told Brian about the mysterious phone call she had received that morning.

"Interesting. Lucky for you, I have some connections I never told you about before that might help. I'm connected to a small network of hobby detectives. We are quite skilled at hacking into computers, and we were able to get into some police files."

Emily sat down. "I don't understand anything you're saying right now. What are you even talking about?"

"I entered your librarian's name and all the facts about the case we have so far."

"Entered his name where? What do you mean 'hacking'? Brian, are you doing something illegal?"

Brian chuckled. "Only a bit, and I *do* operate with strict principles, Emily. I would never alter files or change records. I merely look for details that are already in the system."

Emily was trying to picture Brian as a computer hacker. Apparently she didn't know him as well as she had thought. "How long have you been doing this?"

"In general, for years. In terms of this particular case, I'd say about two days."

She shook her head in an attempt to recalibrate her image of him. "What have you found out?"

"Let's start with something I've already talked to you about. Remember that case we heard about on the nightly news a while ago in South Dakota? The one with the three teens accused of killing that old man? Well, along with three other hobby detectives, we steered the police to the old man's granddaughter. She wanted his money and would stop at nothing."

"Brian, this is all very confusing. I had no idea that you were involved in this type of thing."

Brian laughed. "It isn't something I go around bragging about. It's not exactly kosher work we're doing."

"How do you do this?"

"Well, in the South Dakota case, we just helped ourselves to some police records, and then we brainstormed together a bit. One of the guys on our team is an ex-cop, so he knows his way around the system. Plus, he had a little inside help. Once we figured things out, we simply left a little message where someone higher up would find it, and the police took credit for the rest."

Emily really wished she had a cigarette right now. "Why didn't you tell me you helped solve that case? When we heard about it, you never mentioned those details."

"Emily, if you knew everything about me, I'd run out of bait to keep reeling you in." He paused briefly before continuing in a more serious tone. "Besides, it's not exactly legal breaking into police records. We hacker gumshoes have an unwritten rule to keep quiet about our work. Even with our closest friends and relatives. Until now there was no real reason to share my illicit activities with you. But with recent developments, it seemed like the right time. I'll call you later when I have more information. And, Em? It goes without saying that you shouldn't share this with anyone."

As she hung up the phone, Emily realized she had underestimated Brian. What else didn't she know about him?

* * *

Emily spent the next day working in the office. She needed to collect herself. If Gloria and Brian were right, then she really was considered a prime suspect in the murder case. How could she be caught in the middle of this? And how could she extricate herself? She pulled out paper and a pen from her desk and started to jot down everything she knew about the case so far.

A knock on the door jolted Emily out of her thoughts. It was Mark.

"Hey, Em, have you completely lost your mind?"

Still preoccupied by the new realization that she was not only a "person of interest," but a primary suspect, Emily slowly turned toward Mark. "What? What are you talking about?"

"Only one of the most important meetings of the year, apart from your own tenure track meeting. Everyone waited for you for forty minutes before we finally held the meeting without you."

Emily stood up quickly and knocked over her chair. "Oh my God, I completely spaced it out. The preliminary tenure-review protocol meeting."

"Yes, it is very clear that you forgot. Professor Szongas isn't all that forgiving either. He even implied that you don't care enough about other people's tenure to attend the meeting. He made some crack about your being too concerned with your own meeting in five weeks that you couldn't find the time to attend the general departmental meeting on tenure."

Emily knew she had blown it, but she couldn't hide her disdain for Szongas. "That jerk. He's always trying to sully my reputation. I don't know what he's got against me, but I have felt it ever since I arrived here almost six years ago. Sometimes I think it's because I'm a woman and other times because I'm younger than he is and more progressive."

Mark gestured toward the hallway. "Whatever the case may be, Emily, you'd better get your act together and go apologize to him right now."

As Emily pulled her papers together and tossed them into her bag, Mark said, "By the way, I wouldn't get all high and mighty about gender and age here. Szongas hates anyone who doesn't toe the line. He's like a hard-line communist. Follow the boss or risk the consequences. I don't think your sex and age are related to what's going on here."

Emily still believed that Szongas was a misogynist, but now wasn't the time to debate that point. She moved to stand up. "I better go talk to the shark right now."

Just then there was a knock on her half open door. Szongas. "Emily, may I come in, please?"

Mark quickly excused himself, and Emily was left alone with Szongas. Her voice caught in her throat. "Of course, Professor. Please come in. I'm terribly sorry about this morning. Please forgive me. Things have been crazy lately, and I just haven't been thinking straight."

Szongas slowly closed the door behind him and turned to face Emily. "Emily, I know you work very hard, and I realize you are a dedicated member of this profession. You are even starting to be known internationally. But if you don't show a little more respect for the professional well-being of other members of this department, the consequences will be obvious. Bear this in mind in the future when you make decisions to attend or not to attend certain meetings." He turned and left the room before Emily had a chance to reply.

Emily slumped over her desk and put her head in her hands. She was still in that position when Mark returned. "Uh-oh," he said, "What's it like to swim in shark-infested waters?"

"Please don't make jokes, Mark. This guy's definitely out for blood—no pun intended. Honestly, he doesn't like me. Never has, probably never will. God only knows why." She still thought it had to do with her gender or age.

Mark came around her desk and rested his hand on her shoulder. "C'mon. I'll buy lunch. Pastrami on rye sounding good right about now?"

Emily lifted her head and attempted a feeble smile. "Sure, why not?"

Later that afternoon, Brian called Emily with his latest findings. "Well, it looks like they haven't had any luck pinning this on anyone yet, but they seem eager to close this case. From what I can tell, they've been poking around a certain music professor's business."

"Oh great, Bri. That's all I need. You wouldn't believe the day I've had."

Brian paused before continuing. "Well, it could be getting better. I've been doing my due diligence, and according to police records, it seems that Hansen's ex-wife isn't exactly without a motive."

"What do you mean?"

"Apparently she was named as the beneficiary of Hansen's life-insurance policy. Take a guess how much that was worth."

"How much?"

"Five hundred thousand dollars."

Emily stared at the phone for a moment. "I don't understand. They were divorced. Why would he make her a beneficiary?" A light went on in her eyes. "You don't think …"

"Anything's possible, Em. Just think about that old man's granddaughter."

* * *

THIRTEEN

The next few days Emily had little time to think about murdered librarians. With her tenure-track review only five short weeks away, it was all she could do to get organized. Everything for that review needed to be submitted three weeks prior to the review, and unfortunately, she had spent the last six months preparing classes, teaching, grading papers, and working on her conference presentation. She had had little time to stay on top of things, and her desk was covered in papers, notes, and books. She had finally decided to hire a graduate assistant to help her organize her papers and office and put together her dossier. Natalia, a former student in Emily's Survey of Twentieth-Century Music course, had proven to be more than a little efficient and organized. Emily was hoping Natalia could help her pull everything together for her upcoming tenure meeting. The dossier would need to be submitted within two weeks if she was to be considered for tenure for the upcoming year.

Natalia walked into Emily's office just as Emily was thinking about her. She was carrying a manila envelope in her hand. "Uh, Professor Thurgood … uh, Emily … I found something I think you might want to see."

Emily put down her pen and looked up at Natalia. "What have you got there?"

Natalia pulled a chair close to Emily's desk. She sat down and handed Emily the sealed manila envelope. Emily noticed her own name in careful cursive writing on the outside of the envelope. She reached out to take it. "What is that, Natalia?"

Natalia shook her head. "I have no idea, but it was mixed in with the giant pile of papers you threw into a box for me to organize. It's still sealed, so I assume you haven't seen it yet?"

Emily wondered briefly about Natalia's use of the phrases "giant pile of papers" and "thrown into a box." Was that how Natalia saw Emily's life? It also struck Emily as ironic that her professional fate rested in a cardboard box. What kind of statement was that?

Emily had never seen the envelope before and wondered how it had landed on her desk in the first place. Could this be the mysterious something that someone had left for her? She asked Natalia where it had been in the pile of papers. Perhaps she could place it in a timeline of her life that way. Natalia shrugged her shoulders. "Somewhere between your notes from a course you taught last semester and a conference paper you wrote last year, I guess. Having said that, though, I guess it could have slid in between any of the papers on your desk." Natalia cleared her throat and fiddled with a pen on Emily's desk. "Um, I'm afraid I didn't sense a lot of intuitive organization there."

Emily felt her face flush red. She lifted a loose corner of the envelope where it had been sealed and wiggled her index finger underneath. She tried to open the envelope carefully, but her fingers were shaking, and the paper tore in her hands. She opened the top of the envelope and peered inside. It seemed to be a single sheet of paper.

She reached into the envelope and pulled out the paper. It seemed to be a clumsily sketched note staff with a single page of a musical piece written out by hand. She reached into the envelope again, but it was empty. No other letter or message for her to read. Emily took the envelope in her hand again and examined it carefully, turning it over as she looked for some kind of message. She saw nothing but her name. Someone had written it in cursive in black ink. The *E* on her name was old-fashioned—very curly and ornate. The writing was clean and neat; someone had clearly taken the time to write her name very carefully … which made her wonder about the lack of any other message or note for her. Who would take the time to leave her a single sheet of paper and write her name very carefully without including an explanation of what was in the envelope? Was this the music she was supposed to look to?

Natalia was staring at her. Waiting. "Well, what is it? Does it need to go into your tenure dossier?"

Emily didn't want to mention the mysterious phone call she had received and decided to focus on the matter at hand. "Well, if I had to guess, I'd say it was a sheet from a musical composition, but I couldn't say what or when it is from or who might have left it for me." She turned then to the page of music and examined it with the same scrutiny that she had looked at the envelope. The writing was faded—Emily guessed it was fairly old. It had also been written in pencil, so the markings were not all equally clear. She set the page down, reached into her desk, and pulled out her thin cotton gloves and an extra-powerful magnifying glass that she often used in archives for examining old manuscripts and music closely. She wanted to be careful not to let the oil from her fingers touch the paper too much. Emily held the magnifying glass over the top left side of the page. The piece started in the key of G—that much Emily was sure of; Emily moved the magnifying glass over the notes and bar line, and she saw that the piece clearly modulated to the key of B. Emily noticed some faint letters written on the side of the page: *H, N, D …* What did they mean? And then she thought she saw a name on the top right side of the page. She pushed the page on her desk toward Natalia. "Tell me if you can read that name." She gave Natalia the magnifying glass and pointed to the name on the top-right corner of the page.

Natalia squinted and ran the glass over the sheet of paper. "Hmmm. It's tough to say. It's really hard to read because it is so faded, but I would have to guess Hanna? No, wait—I think it's Anna. I think that H is actually a K, and there's a period after it. K. Anna?"

Emily nodded. "I thought the same thing." She tapped her pencil on the desk. "Natalia, it looks like we have ourselves a mystery. Who left this for me? And when? What does it mean? And most importantly, who could this K. Anna be?" Emily looked at Natalia. "Thanks for bringing this envelope to my attention. Would you please continue sorting and organizing my papers into a meaningful portfolio for my tenure review? You can probably find many of my publications from electronic sources. Just keep track of your hours, and let me know what I owe you for your work."

Emily picked up the phone and glanced briefly at Natalia. "Let me know if you need anything else from me as you work. I need to make a few calls now."

Something was nagging at Emily. The sheet of music on her desk reminded her of something she had found while doing research for her book *The Will to Compose*. She couldn't quite put her finger on what was bothering her, so she leaned back in her chair, closed her eyes and visualized herself in Prague. Two years earlier she had spent an entire year pounding the pavement for musical clues in Prague. Unlike other well-established musical archives around the world, there still was no formal archive dedicated to the music that had been composed and performed in Terezin from 1941 to 1945. Before she'd gone to Prague, she had diligently done research to compile a list of the names of everyone who had been interred at Terezin. Then she had narrowed down the list by making a list of those who she thought might have been actively involved in the musical culture at the camp. It had been painstakingly slow work, but she had been determined to make the cultural contributions and emotional courage of the inmates known to the world. She had pored over transport lists. Sometimes there had been only one or two names out a thousand who had survived the trips eastward, and Emily had fought back tears imagining the anguish and horror of those transports. She had read one account that stated that out of 43,879 people moved eastward in those early years of transports, only 228 had survived. It had been psychologically difficult to go through the lists and documents of those who had perished at the camp, but she'd often thought about what the prisoners had had to face. She'd had to go on. And occasionally she'd also found a name of a survivor.

Those moments gave her hope and made her even more determined to bring the lost voices of Terezin to light. Once she'd had a preliminary list of people who had made musical contributions to the camp, Emily then had had to figure out the addresses of the survivors (of which there were precious few) and those of the families of the survivors. Once she had finished her research of names and addresses, she'd compiled carefully worded letters and sent them en masse to Prague. She'd had no idea what to expect as she'd patiently waited for responses—she had never used such an unorthodox field-research approach. Emily had been surprised when over twenty-five letters had returned. Some of the letters had had little to offer in the way of musical evidence—the families had no documentation to offer Emily that their relatives had composed or performed music in Terezin. But those families had been without exception grateful for Emily's interest in their family members, and a few had even invited her to stay with them when she got to Prague.

In the end, Emily had received a total of ten letters from relatives of inmates or survivors themselves with information about their music. Without exception, each and every one of them had offered Emily the chance to examine the papers and music when she got to Prague. Emily's spirits had been lifted when she'd received these invitations. She'd known that her research was valuable but that it would inevitably also bring up feelings and emotions that many survivors and families had long since tried to push away. It would not be easy for any of them to revisit that terrible time. It had been with the acceptance of the seriousness of her task that Emily had compiled her final list of addresses and put together an itinerary for her research year in Prague.

Emily had applied for and received a grant from the National Endowment for the Arts, so she had not needed to worry about finances while she was in Prague. She'd had enough money coming in to pay her rent for a year, along with funds for utilities, food, and even an occasional cultural outing. With what was left over, Emily had hoped to start a fund for a formal archive for the music of Terezin.

The "archives" Emily had visited at that time were all makeshift; they had been in private basements and attics, in boxes and closets. Before she'd arrived, the families had done their best to collect everything they could find from that horrific time and get it ready for Emily's visit. Inevitably, Emily had been greeted with freshly made pastries and hot coffee, open doors and hearts, and appreciation for her hard work. But behind that loving enthusiasm, Emily had also detected profound sadness and loss.

* * *

Emily kept her eyes closed as she tried to visualize the list of names that she had compiled from that time. There had been ten primary names, and then she'd had another secondary list of names of individuals whom she would visit—not to examine musical documentation from that time, but to get a better sense of the human drama that had unfolded in Terezin. Reading about the horrors of the Holocaust in books was necessary for Emily to understand what had happened, but actual contact with survivors and their family members, along with the relatives of the deceased, was necessary to give her a deeper understanding of that time and what the prisoners had had to endure. She reviewed that list in her mind now—hoping for a clue to the page on the desk in front of her.

Emily then mentally reviewed the ten homes she had visited. She sat quietly at her desk and pictured each experience she had had in Prague. One family had led her to an attic, where she'd sat on the floor and worked her way through cardboard boxes of photographs and scraps of sheet music. Another man, a janitor at a local high school, had shown her a small folder filled with dusty papers with music scribbled on them.

She tried to find the clue to what was nagging at her. Where had she seen something similar to the sheet of music that now lay on her desk? Was she just imagining a connection? She didn't remember anyone named Anna or K. Anna or even Anna K. from her research and time in Prague. But it was always possible that whoever this composer was had not written much or had simply gone under the radar during Emily's initial research phase.

Emily opened her eyes and turned back to the paper on her desk. She put her gloves back on and examined the paper carefully. There was something about the paper itself that she now noticed. It was a bit yellow, that was true, but all paper yellowed with time. There was something else here. Something about the quality of the paper. It was thicker than the paper of today and clearly had a higher acid content. As she examined the paper on her desk more closely, she was reminded of the third and fourth families she had visited. They had shown her choral and chamber music from Terezin. Choir music, chamber music for three instruments or four, transcribed songs from the Yiddish tradition ... Emily now realized that the paper that those composers had used to write their music was similar to the paper on her desk. It must be from Terezin. Emily was almost sure of it now. The question that remained was who had composed it. And more importantly, who had left it for her, and how might it be connected to Hansen's death?

* * *

FOURTEEN

Natalia did an amazing job of helping Emily organize everything for her upcoming tenure review into several three-ring binders; she even prepared bookmarked and text-readable electronic PDF copies of everything for the committee. The tenure-review checklist was located on the first page for easy access, and Natalia had inserted tabs for all the remaining required categories. Emily then provided Natalia with all the necessary documents—two copies of all manuscripts accepted for publication; copies of all previous publications; Emily's PhD dissertation; original copies of student evaluations; a letter with the dean's approval for tenure review; a letter from the department chair; her letter of appointment at the university; a statement of her research, teaching, and service plans for the subsequent five years; her curriculum vitae; a complete list of all courses taught; a statement of her teaching philosophy; proof of consistent and quality service to the university; and many other documents certifying that Emily was a worthy candidate for tenure. With Natalia's help, Emily somehow managed to make the review committee's deadline. She now had three weeks to wait while the committee reviewed all her documentation.

There was nothing more for her to do but wait. Emily opened her laptop and turned it on. She needed to book a flight to Prague.

Emily's plane landed at six thirty on a Friday morning. She had never been able to sleep on flights, and this one had been even more difficult than most. A young family with two small children had sat right behind her on the plane, and the constant thumping of feet against the back of her seat had left no opportunity for dozing. And Emily wasn't one for sleeping in a seated position anyway. Who could sleep sitting up?

There was something abnormal about that. Heads needed to be down on pillows. Blankets needed to cover horizontal bodies, and for God's sake, who could close their eyes and actually fall asleep next to a complete stranger, let alone two rambunctious four-year-olds who were high on sugar?

And so it was that Emily felt an immediate need for sleep upon the plane's landing. Luckily she had a place to stay and could rest for a few hours before starting her work; her friend Pavel had invited her to stay with him while she was in Prague. They had become close friends on her first visit to Prague; he had not only opened his heart and home to her, but he had also shown her around the city.

As she waited to leave the plane, Emily thought about the first time she had gotten to know Pavel. Two years before, Pavel had escorted her to Old Town (Staré Město), the Charles Bridge (Karlův most), and the main sites of Jewish Prague—the Jewish Quarter with its thirteenth-century synagogue and the Old Jewish Cemetery with layers of graves up to twelve feet deep.

Emily pulled her carry-on bag down the aisle of the plane, and as she shuffled off the plane with hundreds of other people, she let her mind wander back to one of the most moving days she had experienced in Prague two years before. Pavel had told Emily he would pick her up at her apartment around ten in the morning, and they would then walk together to the Pinkas Synagogue. Emily had had a late night of reading and writing and had had to force herself out of bed to be ready in time for Pavel. She'd brewed some strong black coffee and waited for him to arrive.

As they'd walked to the synagogue, Pavel had told Emily about his grandfather. He had never met his grandfather personally, because he had died in one of the many transports from Terezin to Auschwitz, but the stories of his grandfather's creative spirit and tenacity in the face of desperate circumstances had been passed along to his children and grandchildren. As Emily and Pavel had approached the synagogue, their talk slowly had switched to the children of Terezin. Pavel had explained to Emily that the artistic culture had not been restricted to music and theater but had extended all the way down to the children of the camp, who had spent much of their precious and rare free time drawing pictures. Some children had drawn pictures of a better time while others had put onto paper what their nightmarish visions of life had become.

Emily thought now about her first time walking through the doors of the Pinkas Synagogue and seeing some of those pictures on the walls. The synagogue had been officially dedicated to the Czech victims of the Holocaust and also protectively housed drawings from the children who had lived in Terezin during that horrific time. Emily had slowly walked around the exhibit, stopping at each drawing so she could examine each carefully. One drawing realistically showed a guard escorting a group of people. Another portrayed a family dressed in their best clothes sitting in a living room and listening to two people performing music on violins.

One particularly moving picture for Emily had been a black-and-white etching of the layout of the camp complete with main building and all the barracks. At the top of the page, the artist—a young child—had drawn a large sun with long rays shooting out from it. Despite the apparent brilliance of the sun, Emily had been able to see that the sun's face was unsmiling and dark clouds hovered over the top of the sun, as if an impending storm were coming. Emily had been struck by another picture that was a close-up of lines of barbed wire. In between the lines it was possible to see single faces trying to look through the wires, but over the front of the faces, the child artist had drawn numbers: 1, 2, 3, 4, 5, 6, 7, 8. The children's lives were literally numbered. Pavel had held Emily's hand as they'd slowly walked past each picture.

Emily could see Pavel now. He was there waiting for her when she got off the plane. She saw him immediately and lifted her hand in a wave; there was no mistaking the signature dark-red beret that he wore at an angle. He was sporting a goatee as well—that was a new development, and Emily noticed that he was wearing a black bow tie. Also a new change. Emily would be sure to compliment him on how his new facial hair framed and complimented his handsome Czech face.

Pavel waved to Emily and motioned for her to join him. He embraced her as he would a long-lost family member, asked her how her flight had been, and told her he had prepared homemade bread and a hearty goulash for her at his apartment in the city.

Nothing sounded better to Emily. If she knew Pavel, there was sure to be beer or wine involved as well, and Emily looked forward to an early evening filled with drink, good food, and a chance to catch up with a dear friend on all that they had missed in each other's lives over the past two years. Of course, they had been keeping in touch by e-mail, phone, and most often, Skype, but nothing could replace a face-to-face get-together for the details of life.

As they drove to Pavel's apartment, he told her that his grandfather's work had recently been published and performed at local concerts in Terezin. Emily gave him another quick hug and told him how thrilled she was to hear that her previous trips to Prague had actually led to a real revitalization effort to perform the music of Terezin.

As Pavel opened the door to his apartment, Emily was hit by a rush of smells: allspice, onions, paprika, tomatoes, nutmeg, cloves, and cinnamon. It was almost too much to bear, and Emily felt an almost immediate reaction from her nose to her stomach, which growled loudly the second she entered his apartment. Pavel laughed and told Emily it wouldn't be long. He told her to make herself comfortable, and then he disappeared into the kitchen to finish the final preparations.

They took their time eating, and Emily surprised herself by having two large bowls of goulash along with three slices of bread. She washed the whole thing down with two bottles of Budvar, the delicious beer Emily had missed so much since her last visit. She wiped her mouth and laughed out loud. "Pavel, you will make me fat!"

Pavel shook his head and gave Emily a sweeping appraisal from head to toe. "Impossible, my friend. You are perfect." Emily blushed and asked Pavel if he could show her the recent publications of his grandfather's music.

They moved to the sofa, where Pavel handed Emily a piece of music from a thin stack of publications. Emily took it in her hand carefully. On the cover of his grandfather's dynamic choral work *From the Cradle to the Grave*, Emily could see red flowers in a field. Emily let her eyes follow the path of flowers; they led directly to the gates of Terezin, along with the now-famous words that had been posted at the gates of many concentration camps: *Arbeit macht Frei*, which Emily knew to mean

"Work sets you free." The letters of the title were all in black, except for the word *grave*, which was in bright-yellow letters. She wondered if the red roses were in reference to the flowers that had been planted before the famous—or infamous—Red Cross visit. She shuddered when she thought about what she had learned about the Red Cross visit; the inmates at Terezin had had to prepare for the visit by planting flowers and trees, by painting downtrodden buildings, by cleaning up the barracks, and by fixing the toilets. The Nazis had wanted the Red Cross to believe that Terezin was a happy place—a place where the Jews could feel safe from the savageries of war. Emily now also remembered that the gates to Terezin had been painted bright yellow right before the official International Red Cross visit. That was it. It was the perfect color for the word *grave*.

Tears filled her eyes, and Emily gave Pavel another quick hug. "This is so amazing. I am so very happy to see your grandfather's work and his legacy come to light again."

Pavel held Emily at arm's length and looked her directly in the eye. "Emily, it is because of you and your efforts that his work has been published and is being performed now. You have done so much for the remembrance effort."

Emily smiled and shook her head. "I have done nothing, Pavel. This music is vital for the world to hear and know. What kind of place would this world be if we forgot?"

Pavel asked Emily what she was hoping to find on her trip to Prague. She got out her list of names and scanned images of other musical pieces she had discovered on her first visit. She then showed Pavel a scanned image of the single sheet of handwritten music that someone had left for her and how she had deduced that it must have also come from Terezin. Pavel scratched his head and asked how she could be so sure that she had music from that time and that location. He said, "You were extremely diligent, and we passed the word around Prague as well. I find it hard to believe that you missed anything during your first visit. And who on earth would be interested in anonymously slipping it under your door?"

Emily then told Pavel everything. She started with her conference and moved on to what had happened with the librarian, Hansen. She told him how Hansen had wanted to show her something but had never had the chance. Then she moved on to the strange phone call with the mysterious message about solving Hansen's murder by looking to music …

Pavel interrupted her and asked, "And you think that the piece of music someone left you is somehow related to Hansen's death?"

Emily slowly nodded. "I think someone left this for me to find. If that mysterious voice was right, this music is directly linked to Hansen's death. And if I am right, it is also connected to Terezin and perhaps even to one of the prisoners there."

As she told Pavel about her past several months, she felt she was unraveling like a piece of yarn that catches on a hook and begins to loosen itself from the rest of the sweater. Once it started, there was no stopping it from coming undone. So much had been happening lately: the murder of a librarian, the suspicion by the police that she had had something to do with it, her tenure review, strange phone calls, and even the illegal computer hacking that her boyfriend had been involved in. Pavel shook his head. "Emily, this all seems a bit, uh … how shall I put it? I think the English word is paranoid? Is that right?"

Emily laughed and was brought back to the present. She knew it sounded far-fetched, but she was beginning to wonder if there might be a connection between her work in Prague and Terezin and Hansen's death after all. Could there be a link? And if so, what could it be? Maybe she was here to find more than the identity of the composer whose work had landed on Emily's desk.

FIFTEEN

The next morning Emily felt refreshed and ready to start solving her mystery. She had left the original page of the music in her locked desk in Wisconsin, but she had brought a high-quality copy to refer to during her time in Prague. She had already shown it to Pavel. Now she wanted to take it to one of the survivors of Terezin who had been active as a musician and composer—Benjamin Bachmann. Bachmann had written many choral works and a few chamber music pieces while at Terezin. He had also been tasked with keeping the music room organized and neat and with helping arrange concerts and other cultural events. He had been of invaluable help on Emily's first visit to Prague and had helped her expand her list of musicians who had been held at the camp.

His grandson, also named Benjamin Bachmann, had also been very helpful when Emily had spent a year in Prague. Like his grandfather, he was also a musician—a pianist—and was very well connected in the current cultural scene in Prague.

The elder Bachmann was expecting her at his apartment at three o'clock sharp. Emily had brought a map of Prague with her, but she was surprised at how easily she was able to remember how to navigate her way to Bachmann's small apartment on Jeruzalemska Street, which was very close to the Jubilee Synagogue. "Jubilee" had always seemed a strange name for a synagogue to Emily, but it was also a name that she could remember easily, and it was a great marker for finding Bachmann's apartment. As she made her way through the winding streets and alleys of Prague, a light rain began to fall, and she pulled her thin jacket closer around her neck. She wasn't one for umbrellas, but she thought now that she should probably have packed one.

Bachmann already had the door open for her as she approached his building. They hugged briefly—Bachmann seemed thinner and frail to Emily—and he invited Emily inside for coffee and the traditional *ovocne knedlicky*, sweet fruit dumplings, that he had just purchased fresh from the local bakery. The coffee was exactly as Emily had remembered it: a small thimble filled with a richly dark, hot liquid. Delicious. The *knedlicky* were tender, and as Emily took her first bite, a gush of warm fruit was released into her mouth. The taste and texture took her back to the last time she had been in Prague, and she realized how quickly she had forgotten how certain foods could release memories.

They finished their dessert and coffee, and as Emily carried the dishes to the kitchen, Bachmann asked her how he could help her. She kept the details leading up to her visit short, focusing instead on the mysterious envelope that had been left for her and how she had deduced that it must have come from Terezin and one of the composers who had been interred there.

"You say it's a female composer?" Bachmann stood up and slowly made his way to a tall shelf of books. The years had been hard on him, and he seemed much older than Emily remembered. He carefully ran a finger across the bindings of the books until he found an unbound manuscript, which he pulled from the shelf. He hummed softly to himself as he thumbed through the pages.

"Benjamin? What are you looking for?" Emily sat on the edge of her seat. If anyone could help her solve this mystery, it was this man in front of her now.

He told Emily to give him a few minutes, and then he visibly withdrew into himself. His eyes took on a distant darkness as he flipped through the pages of the manuscript. He ran a finger down each page, frequently stopping to sigh or make soft noises to himself. A photograph caught his attention, and his finger stopped on the page. He looked up at Emily and nodded. "Yes, here it is. I thought I could find her here."

Emily stood and went to where Bachmann stood. He handed her the manuscript and slowly made his way to a large wooden desk, where he pulled hard on a jammed drawer. It popped open, and he took out a magnifying glass. "You will need this."

She placed the manuscript on the desk and ran the magnifying glass slowly over the picture. "What am I looking for?" Emily looked up at Bachmann, whose gaze had already wandered to the window and beyond. Into the nearby trees? Or further yet—into the past?

Bachmann glanced at Emily and motioned in the air with his hand. "Just see if you recognize anyone in the picture—from our talks the last time you were in Prague."

Emily looked at the picture again. It was a group of prisoners from Terezin. They were standing in a group, and a guard was posing with them. Emily looked closer and thought she could see Rafael Schächter, the composer and conductor. And was that Felix Steinitz? The photo was faded, which made it difficult to make out faces clearly. There were others standing nearby, but Emily didn't recognize them. "Is that Schächter and Felix Steinitz? I don't recognize the others."

"No?" Bachmann came closer now and took the manuscript from Emily. "Let me have another look." He scrunched up his face and held out his hand for the magnifying glass. "I was sure I saw her there."

"Who?" Emily looked over Bachmann's shoulder as he very slowly moved the glass over the paper. The magnifying glass stopped, and he pointed at a woman in the center of the group.

"There. There she is. It is Anna Katz."

A shiver traveled up Emily's arms. Anna Katz? She thought about the sheet of music with the name K. Anna on the top-right corner of the page. Could this possibly be the same woman who had written the mysterious piece of music? "Bachmann, who is this Anna Katz? What can you tell me about her?"

Bachmann's silence was deafening. He ran a hand through his hair and moved to the window, where he slowly paced back and forth. Emily waited patiently for him to answer. She felt a deep sadness for what he had been made to go through back then but also a deep sadness for being the catalyst for his suffering today. He slowly stopped pacing and turned to her. "Emily, what I know about her is this: she was a remarkable woman." His voice broke, and he went back to the window, where he leaned heavily against the frame and looked out at the now-tired garden. He continued speaking without looking at Emily. "She helped direct the women's choir at the camp. She was always ready to help, even though she was as starved and tired as the rest of us." He took a deep breath and sighed. "Anna didn't make it like I did. She was sent on a transport after a music performance—I remember it was the Verdi Requiem—and she died in Auschwitz." Bachmann turned to Emily, and she could see the heavy sadness in his eyes. "She died there, along with thousands of others. They sent her on the train."

Emily's throat felt thick. She reached out to touch Bachmann's arm and told him how sorry she was. For Anna, for him, for all of them. He waved a hand through the air, as if trying to push the past back into the past. He then shook his head and said to her, "It is over. Now let me look at that page you brought with you."

Emily reached into her bag and pulled out the copy she had carried with her from Wisconsin. She was upset with herself for not bringing the original now. She had wanted to preserve the original document, but maybe Bachmann could have gleaned more from the authentic page. *Too late now,* she thought as she handed him the single sheet of paper.

He took it gently, as if it were a newborn baby, and asked Emily for the magnifying glass. "My old eyes are not what they once were," he said quietly. He walked to the desk without a sound and sat with the paper, the magnifying glass, and his thoughts.

Emily did not interrupt him during the forty-five minutes that he pored over the page. She was in no hurry as she sat quietly and waited, trying not to stare at him and not wanting to disturb his concentration while he studied the notes. As he examined the page, he would hum or sigh again and again. A few times Emily could feel him suddenly holding his breath, as if to keep a fleeting memory from passing, before releasing the air in a rush of sound.

After some time, Bachmann looked up from his desk and noticed Emily, as if for the first time. He ran a hand through his disheveled hair and said to her in a quiet voice, "It is all I can do for today. Can you return tomorrow? I am very tired now. This may or may not be Anna's writing, but I cannot do more today."

Emily stood quickly and went to him, putting her hands on his shoulders from behind to massage the kinks that had formed over the past hour. "Bachmann," she said in a hushed voice, "I am so sorry I bothered you with this. I can see how it wears on you, and I am deeply sorry." Bachmann shook his head before turning to look her in the eye. "No, I am sorry. Sorry that it was she and not I who went to Auschwitz that day." Emily left him with his thoughts and memories.

* * *

Sixteen

August 1943

Anna had to cajole the women back to practicing the Verdi Requiem. As their leader, she was in charge of their musical development, but she also felt responsible for their psychological well-being. Playing and singing for their friends' transport to the east had been more than most of them could bear, and Anna was worried about their spirits breaking in two. And the worst thing Anna could imagine was to see her friends and herself give in to "Auschwitz disease," where the spirit was broken before the body. Anna had seen it before: when the soul was crushed, people simply gave up and stopped functioning socially. They wore their despair like a cloak and could recover only with great difficulty, if at all.

The only hint of a treatment Anna knew for this condition was music. A simple melody, a familiar song, a less-than-perfect instrument on which to play a few notes—these small things carried a significance virtually impossible for those to understand who had never experienced the horrors of life in a concentration camp. And despite the fact that it was a requiem they were practicing, it was the joy that music could give that Anna wanted the women to remember. She tried to remember now what Schächter had said to them at their very first rehearsal. What was it? Ah, yes: "We will sing to the Nazis what we cannot say to them."

Many of the inmates were against singing the Christian music of Verdi and argued that Jews should not be singing a Christian mass but should be singing Jewish and Yiddish folk songs or other classical music instead. Schächter remained adamant about rehearsing and performing Christian music to Christians and believed that they might be able to force the Nazis to come to their senses in the process. Because Schächter had made Anna the musical leader of the women's group, he'd pulled her aside to point out the key elements in Verdi's music that he wanted to emphasize in their performances. He kept his voice low so the guards couldn't hear him, and he explained to her that the text to Verdi's Latin Catholic Requiem was filled with stark and dramatic images of hell and pictures of people crying over loved ones who had gone to hell. He turned to Anna to ask her quietly, "Don't you believe, deep down in your heart, that we can dig down and penetrate the Nazis' moral core with this piece? That we can get them to stop and ask themselves what this madness is that they have created? And what they are really doing here to all of us?"

Anna quietly asked Schächter what might happen if the Nazis truly understood what the inmates were trying to say with Verdi's music.

He touched her hand softly and said, "I think we all know the answer to that, and I understand if there are some among us who would rather not participate. Please talk to the women about this and offer them all a way out of that danger."

Anna spent the first few minutes of her rehearsal time explaining in a quiet voice what Schächter had told her about Verdi's Requiem. She explained to all that reprisals were always a possibility and that she and Schächter completely understood if there were individuals in the group who declined to sing in the choir. She waited for a few minutes for a reaction from the group.

No one moved.

December 1943

Anna rolled onto her side and ran a hand slowly over her rib cage. In the darkness she was able to run a finger through the grooves between her ribs. The bones were pressing against the surface of her skin; trying to survive on the meager scraps of bread and a few potatoes had made all the inmates turn gaunt. Anna couldn't even remember what meat tasted like, but if she closed her eyes very tightly, she could now picture the field of strawberries at her grandmother's farm. She kept her eyes closed and reached out a hand for the berries. Sweet and delicious. Red goodness.

The door to the women's barracks opened, and a female guard entered. Anna opened her eyes and saw a woman's shape in the darkness. It occurred to Anna from the fullness of the woman's hips and thighs that she clearly had enough meat to eat, and Anna imagined reaching out to grab a handful of her fat and stuffing it into her mouth.

The woman approached Anna's bed and told her to sit up. Anna lowered her legs off the side of the bed. The guard then lifted Anna's thin pillow off the bed to reveal a stack of unevenly sized papers. Anna kept very still. How had the guard known that she had been hiding her compositions there? She put her head in her hands and waited. It had only been a matter of time. What would happen now?

The guard lowered her voice. "Anna, look at me. I knew you before this time. Do you remember me?"

Anna looked up. Could it be? Was it really her music composition teacher from the Prague Conservatory—Irena Svobodova? Anna rubbed her eyes and looked again. She whispered, "Pani Profesore?"

The guard nodded. "Yes, it is true. They are forcing me to guard Terezin because of my music background. This has become the model camp for the world to believe all you Jews are comfortable and happy. They need guards with musical talent to help organize the propaganda. You have to understand I do not want to be here any more than you do." The guard touched Anna's shoulder lightly and sighed. "Ah, you are so very thin, Anna."

She looked at Anna and waited. Anna said nothing, so Svobodova said, "I saw you writing the other day, but you didn't notice me. I watched as you hid the sheets under your pillow. Anna, I am not here to hurt you. I want to help you."

Help her? How?

"You were always one of my favorite composition students. Let me take these pages and others as you complete them. I will take them home and hide them carefully. You will get them back when this is all over." At the word *this*, Svobodova made a sweeping gesture of the barracks with her hand.

* * *

Seventeen

January 2014

Emily made the trek back to Pavel's apartment and wondered if there was even a remote chance she could find a pastrami on rye sandwich in Prague. Her nerves could use some calming. She mentally reviewed what she had just learned. Bachmann had identified someone named Anna Katz in an old, faded picture from Terezin. He also seemed to think that she might have written the music that had been left on Emily's desk. He also seemed sure that she had been sent to Auschwitz and had likely not survived.

Emily was sure she would find out more tomorrow, but in the meantime she pondered her next move. It certainly seemed plausible that this Anna Katz could be the same Anna who had composed the music that Emily had left at Bachmann's apartment. Bachmann didn't know if Anna had relatives in Prague who had survived the war. He had told Emily he would go through his papers and documents from that time as well as phone books from the present to see if he could find any leads. But he couldn't help her anymore today. Finding Anna's picture, seeing her again, remembering the dark days of war time—it was all too much for him. From the moment he'd seen Anna's photograph, he had seemed to grow more frail right before Emily's eyes. She could see that she had overspent her time there, and she'd thanked him for his efforts, hugged him one last time, and headed back to Pavel's. Perhaps Pavel could brainstorm with her on what her next step should be.

Emily's thoughts kept travelling back to Anna. If she had indeed perished during a transport to Auschwitz or in the Auschwitz concentration camp, then how could her music have survived? Who might have protected and then saved it in that case? Emily was stuck on this one major question. Perhaps this was the key to unlocking the mystery before her. If she could find the person who had saved Anna's music, then maybe she could also find out more about the connection between Anna, the music, and Hansen's murder ... She knew it wouldn't be easy, but she had to retrace the steps to Anna somehow. And she now had an idea who might be able to help her with that.

* * *

Emily knocked on Pavel's door. She could already smell the *Chessnekova polevka* at the end of the hallway. There was no mistaking the odor of an entire head of garlic, and her mouth started watering before she even entered the apartment. Pavel opened the door and made a sweeping gesture for her to come in. He told her to follow him into the kitchen as he finished dinner preparations. She asked him about the Czech garlic soup recipe while he cooked.

"For starters, there is one whole garlic inside there." He made a gesture with both hands as if he were holding a small ball. "Some chicken sauce ..." Pavel turned from his stirring to look at Emily. "Is this the right word?"

Emily smiled. "Actually, I think you mean 'head of garlic' and 'chicken broth,' but I understand." She leaned over the pot and fanned the garlic smell toward her nose. "What else is in there?"

Pavel explained that the recipe varied from house to house, but that overall it was very simple. He laughed when he told her that was why he enjoyed preparing it so much. He explained the soup was a simple mix of garlic, broth, butter, and sometimes a bit of lemon. Then to top it all off, heavy bread was used to soak in the traditional soup.

Emily polished off three bowls of Pavel's garlic soup along with two Budvar beers and what she guessed was close to half a loaf of bread. She patted her stomach and complained to Pavel that she would have to buy new clothes before leaving Prague. "No, not possible." He shook his head. "It is only water and garlic. It is told that the garlic will even make you thin." He gestured to the soup pot. "You can even have some more." Emily laughed. "Pavel, you sound like an old Czech grandmother!"

Pavel refused to let Emily near the kitchen for cleanup, so she went to her room and plugged in her laptop. She hadn't checked her e-mail since arriving in Prague, and she wanted to make sure she hadn't missed anything that needed immediate attention.

She looked at the long list of unread messages and marked six as priority: two from Brian, three from Mark, and one from Szongas (she groaned out loud when she saw his name in her box).

First, she started with the messages from Brian. She realized with a twinge that she hadn't even called him to tell him that she had arrived safely in Prague. She felt a bit sheepish as she clicked on the first message, dated the previous day. "Have a safe trip. Don't forget to write. Love, Brian." Emily felt a pang in her gut when she read the word *forget*. Truth be told, she hadn't thought about him a single time since boarding the plane in Chicago. She wondered why that was but then told herself to move on to the next message. She absentmindedly clicked on Brian's second message. "Football game would be nice when you come back. Love, Brian." Emily found herself poking the delete key hard with her right index finger. She really hated football, and after yesterday's meeting with Bachmann, football seemed even more banal. The minute the message was gone, though, she felt almost as if she had betrayed Brian by erasing it. Strange. It was only a football game after all. Right?

Pavel knocked softly on the door and asked if she might like some coffee or a beer or maybe something else to drink. She turned from her screen just long enough to tell him she'd love some coffee with cream if he had it and then went back to her e-mail. Mark joked about her "musical mystery tour" and asked how her research was going. He then mentioned that one of their colleagues—Anne Jenkins—had just been denied tenure. Anne's research and performance records were impeccable, and Emily wondered again about Szongas's predilections for male faculty. She was convinced he was nothing but a misogynist but knew that her suspicions would fall on deaf ears with Mark. He told her he felt that Anne had been denied tenure because the current economic strain on the department had left them all trying to cut corners. Mark's own tenure review was scheduled for the following spring, and he had more than once talked to Emily about his fear that he might not be granted tenure and might be out on the street looking for another job soon. Emily couldn't imagine that happening, as Mark was always reinventing himself and offering to teach the courses that no one else wanted to teach, even though they were far outside his area of expertise. She couldn't imagine them letting go of someone who was so willing to take on all the unwanted work in the department; most of the tenured faculty could pick and choose what courses they wanted, and they considered teaching the introductory courses to be like taking out the trash. Mark never hesitated to teach Introduction to World Music or Introduction to Western Music.

He also mentioned that Szongas had been in a foul mood ever since she had left. She wondered at the unstated connection. Could her own tenure be at risk? She noticed then that Mark had sent his messages not through the university system but through his private Gmail account. Smart man. Wouldn't want a tirade of gossip falling into the wrong hands. Emily rolled her mouse over the message from Szongas but found herself hesitating. She had had such a wonderful evening with Pavel and such an emotional day with Bachmann. Could she handle news about her tenure-review results from Szongas now? At that moment, Pavel appeared in the doorway and asked if she'd like to join him for coffee. Saved by the bell. Perfect excuse to avoid Szongas's e-mail. Emily hit the log-off button and shut down her machine. She was far away from the university. Surely whatever it was could wait another day.

As they sipped their coffee, Pavel shared stories of his grandfather with Emily. Even though he had never met him personally, he loved to tell the stories of his grandfather's life. Emily sensed the pride with which he recounted tales that had been passed down to him. It occurred to her that Pavel hadn't talked much about his own life since she had arrived.

Emily reached out and put her hand on his arm. "What about you? Tell me about yourself, Pavel. How have you been these past two years? You haven't mentioned your girlfriend even once."

His face went red. "We are no longer together. Boring story." He stood up and carried the coffee cups to the kitchen. Anna followed him.

"Pavel, what happened? Why didn't you tell me?" Emily was close on his heels as he quickly moved to the kitchen. He kept his back to her as he washed the cups in the sink. He didn't turn around but told Emily that Irena had been the jealous type and couldn't stand the thought of him with another woman. Emily stood behind him and put her hand on his shoulder. "What woman? Were you involved with someone else? You never told me."

Pavel turned around, and they were now face-to-face and inches apart. He avoided her eyes as he whispered, "I wasn't. It was you. She left me because of you."

Emily took a big step backward and stared at Pavel. What on earth did he mean? They had never gotten involved while she had been in Prague two years earlier. Sure, they had flirted occasionally, but neither one of them had ever crossed that invisible line. Emily waited for him to explain.

"Emily." Pavel took a step forward, once again closing the gap between them. "She could see what you meant to me and didn't want to compete with even an unexpressed love." He took her by the arms and pulled her closer. "She left me because of you."

Emily didn't know what to say. She had been so focused on her work, on her own needs and wants, she hadn't paid much attention to what anyone else needed. She looked him in the eye and said, "Pavel, I am so sorry." Then she pulled back and quickly excused herself to go to bed. She needed time to think. When she came out of her room an hour later to talk to him, he was gone. She was alone in the apartment.

* * *

EIGHTEEN

Emily met with the elder Bachmann late the next morning. He had agreed to let Emily bring the treats this time, so she decided to stop at the Paneria, a bakery she had noticed on her last visit to Bachmann close to the metro station Hlavní Nádraží. She kept chanting the name of the metro station to herself rhythmically as she walked to the bakery. Hlavní Nádraží, Hlavní Nádraží, Hlavní Nádraží … It had a musical ring to it. The station was minutes away from Bachmann's apartment by foot, and Emily marveled again at the wonders of city transportation. So many buses and trains. In Madison she had to take her car or walk everywhere, and in the winter, it was a constant challenge to slog through the snow. Here in Prague life seemed to roar on endlessly, and people could always find a way to get where they were going. There was a life to this city that she hadn't felt in a while.

She stepped into Paneria and wondered absentmindedly if it was related to the many Paneras she had seen in the States. The name was very similar, and she noticed now that the offerings also looked like they could be in a shop in Madison or Chicago or in any other U.S. town. Croissants, strawberry tarts, small pastries that definitely looked much classier than donuts. It all looked tasty. She stepped up and used her rusty Czech to order croissants and two small packets of strawberry jelly. She wasn't sure if Bachmann had any jelly in his apartment, and she loved to smear it on croissants. She was definitely not a purist.

Bachmann was again waiting for her when she arrived and greeted her with the same procedure as the day before: a hug, a smile, and a sweeping gesture to follow him into his apartment. He had already set the table; Emily could see a lacy tablecloth, two small porcelain plates, two thimble-sized cups for coffee, and a small knife to the side of each plate. He had already boiled two three-minute eggs, and those had also been placed at the head of the plates in small egg holders. Emily saw the small spoons just to the top of the egg cups and marveled at the detail with which this man did everything. She was in good hands with her musical puzzle, she reflected now. If anyone could suss out the clues for who had written the music, it was going to be Bachmann.

He took her coat and hung it in a small closet by the front door. He led her to the prepared table and invited her to sit. Emily set the croissants on the plates and put a small packet of strawberry jelly by each one. Bachmann looked at Emily questioningly. She responded quickly, "Oh, those are strawberry jelly packets. I guess they are not so common here? I wasn't sure if you had marmalade, so I brought some for us." Bachmann picked up one of the small packets and turned it over in his hand. He chuckled softly to himself. Emily wondered what the joke was and waited for him to say more, but he simply set the jam back down and pulled out a chair for Emily to sit down.

When Bachmann quietly began eating, Emily followed his lead and ate without speaking, enjoying the tastes of butter, jam, coffee, and egg that mixed together and swirled around in her mouth. Delicious. When they had finished, Emily suggested to Bachmann that he relax wherever he wanted; she was going to take care of cleanup today. She was glad when he didn't protest and moved to the living room while she carefully carried the fragile porcelain dishes to the small kitchen. As she washed the dishes in a small sink of warm water, she looked around her. This was the kitchen of a careful man, she thought. Small cotton curtains with tiny floral print hung in front of a small window. The curtains were immaculate, and Emily noticed that the sink, cupboards, and countertops had all been scrubbed to glisten. Exquisite attention to detail. Emily thought about Bachmann's clothing choices as well. Freshly pressed button-down white shirt, probably starched, and black wool pants. His face was cleanly shaven, and every hair was in place. Emily couldn't say the same for herself and wished now that she had taken more care that morning to shower and style her hair. She wiped her hands on the white kitchen towel and attempted to pat down the loose locks around her face. It was the best she could do under the circumstances, but she hoped that Bachmann didn't think less of her for how she looked.

She joined him in the next room, where he had already laid out the music Emily had brought to him the day before. She could feel a quiet energy in the air. It seemed to float around him like a force field. She sensed he had discovered something. She joined him at the table and asked him what he thought.

"I spent many hours last night studying this page. It's a shame you don't have more, Emily. Could you please tell me again how you got this?"

Emily told him about the mysterious envelope and how it had been discovered. She explained that she didn't know what it meant, who had left it, or even who had composed it. She wished she had more information, but she couldn't even say if there was any more to this piece of music or if that was the only page.

Bachmann agreed that they had precious little information to go on, but at least they had the one page to examine. He pushed a second piece of white paper toward Emily and asked her to have a look. She could see that he had made notes for himself as he had studied the music; it was in Czech, and the handwriting was shaky and difficult to read. She had to ask him to read parts of it for her. She could definitely speak enough Czech to order pastries, but handwriting was a challenge.

Bachmann explained that he had analyzed the composition—at least the bits that they had to go on, and had noticed some familiar patterns. He asked her to move with him to a small upright piano in the corner of the room where he set his page of handwritten notes on the music holder. He told her he had pulled out a disguised melody from the music; the notes G, G, B, and A made up the first line. He played these on the out-of-tune piano and hummed along as he pointed to the notes on the paper. Then Bachmann moved to the second line of the melody and hummed it as well: D, F, E-flat. It sounded dissonant to Emily, and she asked him what he thought. Bachmann raised a hand and quietly said, "I will tell you what I think, but I'd like to finish this first." Emily sat without talking while Bachmann opened his mouth wide now and sang as he played the final notes of the melody: B-flat, B-flat, B-flat.

When he turned to Emily, he had tears in his eyes. Emily waited for him to continue. "This is Anna's work, Emily. I am almost certain."

Emily quietly asked him how he could be so sure, and he asked her to move back to the living room with him. He explained that the piano bench was so hard on his bony body and that he preferred the comfort of the overstuffed chairs. He then told Emily what he knew about Anna, and she listened quietly, kicking herself for forgetting to bring the tape recorder she had carried with her all the way to Prague.

"I met her during one of our many choir rehearsals. She was a remarkable woman. Schächter had called us to rehearse, and the men and the women came together for the first time. It wasn't usual for us to rehearse together all the time, so it made a big impression on me to see the women that night.

"Anna was in charge of the women in the group. Schächter had asked her to help him, especially with the Verdi Requiem. It was such a challenge to learn all the music and the lyrics, and Schächter was the only person who had an actual score. There was no way he could feasibly teach all the women everything, so he had asked Anna to help him. She worked with the women constantly—when they were in their barracks, she would quietly sing with them and teach them the text and the music." Bachmann asked Emily if she could fetch him a cold glass of water. When she returned, he was deep in thought. She handed him the glass and waited for him to continue.

"She had a quiet confidence about her." He took a sip of the water. "She knew that singing the Requiem was risky—for her, for Schächter, for everyone. Schächter made it clear that he wanted to sing the Requiem in defiance to the Germans. There was always a good chance that the Nazis would find out what his real intentions were, and if they did, he'd be shot. And the choir members would probably have a similar fate. But Anna also knew that there is a joy to music that can't be found anywhere else. And a salvation in music that cannot be granted by any other authority." Benjamin looked her in the eye. "Few people understand that, Emily. Anna was special. Like Schächter, she wanted to make the hellish life in Terezin more bearable for the prisoners." He took a small sip of water. "And then she started composing."

Emily leaned forward in her seat. "What can you tell me about that?"

"All I can tell you is she was trying to find the best way to fight back—like everyone else there. They couldn't leave Terezin, and they were at the mercy of their captors, but music was what she knew best, so she used those tools to fight the Nazis. Actually, she never really felt like she was fighting the Nazis directly but that she was helping others in the camp fight back and survive through music and hidden meaning."

"Hidden meaning?" Emily somehow felt that Benjamin's next words might help her understand the last few weeks.

"Yes. She used her compositions to hide messages for the prisoners and against the guards in the camp and also against the Germans and the Nazis. A phrase like *'Gebt den Glauben nicht auf!'*" He sang the notes from the first part of the melody he had shown her at the piano.

"Don't give up believing!" He held a fist in the air as he sang the tune again, more loudly this time. "She created that melody from the first notes of each word in that phrase. See here?" Bachmann went to the piano again and played the notes G, G, B, A. Emily asked why Anna had used B for the German word *nicht*.

"Ah, that is her genius. *N* is represented by the Cyrillic sign *H* in Russian, and *H* is musically represented by the note B in the German musical system." He waited to let what he had said soak in.

Emily nodded. This music was more sophisticated than she had originally thought. Bachmann saw that she understood and continued, "She then explained to the other prisoners what she was doing so they would understand the message and gather strength. And each time they all sang the music for the guards at the camp or any other oppressor who was nearby, they would have the shared knowledge that they were singing a revolutionary fighting song."

Anna had clearly been a thoughtful and talented woman. Emily wished she could have met her. She asked Bachmann if he would mind playing the entire piece at the piano for her. Not just the melodies but the entire piece. Bachmann stood and went to the small console. Now that Emily knew the hidden truth behind the music, she felt the power behind the notes. She could only begin to imagine what that had meant for the singers and performers of such music to have any kind of power over their captor's.

When Bachmann finished the short page of music, Emily asked if he knew of other music Anna had composed. He told her that composing had been difficult for her in the camp because conditions had made finding even the most basic resources a challenge. Paper, pencils, and even time had been a scarce resource, as most prisoners had had ten-hour work duty each day followed by evenings when they often had gotten together to sing or perform. Anna would have had to find moments in between everything to sketch out her ideas. And as Bachmann explained, she likely had developed the musical ideas and carried them with her before she would finally have been able to write them down on paper secretively.

Emily still didn't understand how the music could have survived Anna's deportation to the east, and she asked him if he had any ideas about that. He grew quiet. "Well, I do know there was once a man at Terezin who kept a secret diary and hid it in the attic before he was sent to the east. That diary was found by workers who were preparing to turn Terezin into a museum many, many years later, and they published it then. He worked in the camp as a youth organizer or something like that, and he also had to put together lists of people to send to the east." Bachmann's eyes grew dark. "It was a most unenviable task to select the names for transports. He had a great pressure from all sides."

Emily couldn't imagine. Life during the war remained largely abstract for her, but meeting Bachmann, a survivor from that time, made it a bit easier—albeit more painful, to picture what the prisoners had been forced to bear during that awful time. After a moment, Emily asked Bachmann if there could have been another way for Anna's music to survive.

"I do not know that, Emily. If you have the music now, it likely was not left at the camp. Perhaps she gave it to someone when she left the camp?" Emily sensed that Bachmann's energy was fading—the same thing had happened the day before.

"Can you think of anyone who might have been able to help her with that?" Emily was thinking about the tape recorder she had left in her suitcase. Her memory would have to suffice. Then she thought about Anna's memory abilities—and Bachmann's ability to remember the smallest detail from that time. Surely she could remember a single conversation?

"Let me think about that, Emily. I will try to remember the other women in her barracks and will let you know if I remember anything. But now I am tired." Bachmann stood up, and Emily understood that it was time for her to go. She thanked him for his generosity and genius and made her way back to Pavel's apartment.

* * *

NINETEEN

March 1944

Anna could still feel the sharp bones of ribs protruding from her chest when she ran a hand over them, but Pani Profesore had been supplying her for three months with small bits of dried meat each time she came to collect a sheet of music from Anna, and Anna was feeling a bit stronger day by day.

She glanced around the barracks at her fellow inmates. The camp was bursting now; Terezin had only been meant for six or seven thousand people at the most, and Anna was certain that at least five times that number were now crammed into the small camp. Most women had to share a small cot, and more and more prisoners were dying from disease and starvation every day. The few toilets in Terezin were always overflowing, and rats and fleas were everywhere.

Anna looked through the window toward the south side of the camp and saw smoke rising into the air. She could see the smoke every day now. Pani had told her that so many inmates were dying from disease and starvation that, before the end of 1942, the Germans had decided to build a crematorium just to the south of the camp to burn the bodies. She had told Anna that they were able to burn up to two hundred bodies each day.

Anna shuddered at the thought of what their lives had become.

Pani Svobodova approached her now. "Anna, you must come with me. They want to hear Verdi's Requiem in one hour. Please hurry."

They had been losing members of the choir to disease and to transports, and the choir had grown considerably smaller as a result. "I don't think we can do that. We have lost so many singers lately. We don't have enough voices."

Svobodova gestured toward the south of the camp and then to the east. "You can go south. You can go east. Or you can go sing."

Anna stood up to gather the women. "Give me ten minutes to collect everyone and meet us in the music hall. Schächter should go and collect the men."

Schächter and the men were waiting and in formation by the time Anna had gotten all the female singers together. Their group had been at least 140 voices strong when they had started rehearsing the Verdi, but they had lost so many to the transports and to disease. Now their number stood at 95. Anna looked around the group and felt her heart tighten. Schächter caught her eye across the crowd and smiled. She nodded back to him and called the women around her.

"Come together now. Altos here and sopranos over there." She quickly took charge and got everyone into position. As Anna took her place in line with the altos, Schächter organized the men into vocal groups and took his position in front of them as conductor. He alone had a score to read from. It was the only copy in the entire camp. For months Anna had rehearsed with the women by teaching them the complex and lengthy composition one line at a time. Together they'd had to learn the music and the Latin text. Anna wondered briefly if a choir had ever accomplished such a feat before.

Anna looked out at the audience and saw that soldiers, Nazis, and members of the International Red Cross had gathered to hear Verdi's Requiem. She could see now why they had been called to perform. It was another international group visit, and their choral performance was part of an elaborate ruse to fool the outside world into believing that Terezin was a comfortable and safe home for the Jews.

Schächter turned to the audience and announced that this would be their fourteenth performance of Verdi's Requiem at Terezin. "Ladies and gentlemen, we apologize for the legless piano that we will use in place of an orchestra and the smaller-than-normal chorus, but I think you will agree that these beautiful voices need no additional accompaniment." He tapped his hand in the air to set the beat, and the choir began to sing.

* * *

Twenty

January 2014

Pavel was not home when Emily arrived, and she was secretly grateful. Yesterday's encounter had left her shaken and wondering about her own ability to judge relationships. She quickly boiled some water for tea and went to her room to read her e-mail. The message from Szongas was still waiting, but Emily now noticed another new message from a sender she didn't recognize: farandwide44. It was a Hotmail address, so it could be spam. Emily didn't want yet another virus to cripple her computer, so she would be careful not to click on any links, but she did want to see if it was from someone she knew.

Thinking it was probably just junk mail, Emily absentmindedly clicked on it and reached for her tea while the page loaded. Connection speed was slower here, and it gave her plenty of time to take a sip of something hot. When she looked up at the screen, she gasped at the message waiting for her: "How is your trip going? Have you found any answers? Keep looking to the music, and you will find your way."

Emily hit the reply button on her screen and wrote a quick message: "Who are you?" She clicked send and waited. Two seconds passed, and a message popped into her inbox: "Unable to send to farandwide44. Sender unknown."

Emily groaned and slapped the desk with her right hand. This had to be the same person who had called her back in Madison. There was that expression again: "look to the music." But whoever it was seemed intent on concealing his or her identity. Who could it be? Could it be someone she knew? Emily made a mental list of everyone she had told she was going to Prague: Brian, Szongas, Mark, her mother … obviously Pavel and Bachmann … Of course, those people could have passed on that information to anyone else, and Emily could never be sure who knew she was here.

She started writing an e-mail to Brian. He was so good at hacking and making his way into computer databases. Maybe he could help her now. She started writing him a message and then thought better of it and picked up her cell phone. As it started to ring, Emily took a quick look at her watch. She had forgotten the time difference for a moment and hoped she hadn't woken him. She breathed a sigh of relief. It was six. Surely he was awake by now.

Just as she expected, he picked up after three rings. He clearly had just gotten up; his voice was always very scratchy until he had something hot to drink in the morning. "Hello?"

Emily felt a rush of gratitude that he had picked up. The e-mail message from farandwide44 had upset her more than she had thought. In a rush, she told Brian about her first days in Prague, her visits with Pavel and Bachmann, and the discovery that Anna Katz had been the composer of the music left for her in her office.

Brian seemed quiet and distant, and Emily asked him if something was bothering him. He hesitated before replying. "Well, there actually is something, but I'd rather speak to you in person about it."

Emily wondered if he was angry that she hadn't called or written him when she had first arrived. She realized she hadn't even told him when she would be returning.

Brian asked if Emily needed him to help her with anything.

She sheepishly realized that he was able to see right through her real reason for calling. He had immediately recognized that she needed a favor … She almost didn't ask him to help her because she felt so guilty and then thought better of it. She really needed some help.

"Remember how you broke into that computer database and figured out all those things?" She knew she wasn't phrasing this well, but she suddenly felt nervous—beholden.

"Yes, of course. Do you need me to do some cyberdetecting for you?"

It was amazing how Brian could so quickly cut to the chase. He really was true to his efficient nature. She then told him about the mystery caller and asked what he thought.

He didn't answer immediately. When he did, his voice sounded strangely tight. "Why do you always wait to ask me for help, Emily? Don't you trust me? I could've helped you sooner with this if you had put your faith in me more."

Emily suddenly felt defensive and explained that she really did trust him. She didn't understand his sudden anger. She had never really felt as if she was in danger, and the mystery voice had truly led her in the right direction. But now she was beginning to wonder. Someone had an awful lot of information about her whereabouts and actions, and she desperately wanted to know who it was.

She asked him again if he could help. "Do you know how you might find this person, Brian?"

Again, Brian's answer came slowly. This time, though, he sounded resigned. "I will contact my sources and see what they think. We could definitely start with a trace of the call you received that day. There's most likely a way to figure out the telephone number of whoever called you. Can you remember what day it was exactly?"

Emily thought about it. That was the day Natalia had been helping her with the mess of papers on her desk. It had definitely been before her tenure-review meeting … February tenth? Or was it the eleventh? She asked Brian if he could check both those days. She hadn't received many calls to her home phone recently, so it theoretically could be a fairly simple matter to narrow it down. She then remembered the e-mail from farandwide44 and asked Brian how hard it would be to figure out the real identity of an unknown sender.

"That's actually fairly easy. You can do it right from there."

Emily was sure it was more difficult than Brian let on, but she asked him what the necessary steps were. He gave her a number of tips, and, remembering how mad she was at herself for forgetting to take her tape recorder to Bachmann's apartment, she asked Brian to wait a sec while she grabbed a pen, so she could put everything down on paper while she was talking to him.

The first thing Brian suggested was to find the sender's location by locating the IP address in the header of the e-mail message. He walked her through where to find this address on an e-mail message, and then he told her to copy and paste that IP address into a search engine on the website yougettool.com to trace the source of the IP address. She would then be able to at least locate the approximate source location of the e-mail. Emily wasn't sure she understood his directions.

"Brian, are you saying that if I cut and paste a line from someone's e-mail, I can actually find out where the e-mail was sent from?"

"Yes, that is correct. But then you can take it one step further if you want to find out who actually sent the message. If you have the name of the sender—the e-mail address functions as the name in this case—and his or her location, you should be able to get pretty close to finding that person."

Emily asked him to explain how she could find the identity of the sender. She took careful notes as he walked her through the next steps, stopping him often to repeat or rephrase steps she would need to take. He told her to first go to Facebook.com and copy the sender's e-mail address into the Facebook.com search field. Emily had done this type of thing before when she had looked for new "friends" when she had initially set up her own account.

Brian told her this method of searching for her unknown e-mail sender's identity would only be successful if he or she actually had a Facebook account, but, as he also told her, 450 million people had Facebook accounts, so he thought it would be fairly simple to find out who that person was. She could then take it one step further and download the Facebook user's profile picture and do a search of that image on Google images to see if the sender had other additional social network accounts. From those social network accounts, she could find out everything from where the person lived to what he or she had eaten for breakfast.

Emily was having a tough time keeping up with Brian's quick descriptions. This was clearly old hat for him, but she was so busy trying to taking notes that she hadn't said anything while Brian was talking. She now realized he was waiting for her to answer.

"Emily? You still there?"

She put down her pen. "Yes, sorry. I was busy taking notes. I had no idea how transparent all our web activity makes us. It's really scary, isn't it?"

"I suppose it can be rather frightening, especially if it gets into the wrong hands, but it also makes it possible for us to find people if and when we need to do so. Look at it that way." Emily briefly wondered how often he had tracked people this way. He clearly knew his way around cyberspace.

Emily thanked him for his tips and the offer to trace the source of the incoming phone call to her office. She asked him if she could call him back if she ran into a snag. He quietly replied that he might not always be around to help her. As she hung up the phone, she wondered what he meant.

Brian had made cybersleuthing sound so easy, but Emily was having a much more difficult time than she had expected. For starters, she couldn't for the life of her find the IP address on the sender's message. She started with the e-mail address, clicking on the left side of the mouse and then on the right side. Nothing. Then she tried finding other paths to the IP address but only ended up with the most basic user information. She finally noticed a small icon on the upper right-hand corner of the message, which, when she clicked on it, revealed a long list of background information about the message, including the IP address. Emily wanted to jump up and do a victory dance, but she settled on another sip of tea as her reward. It was now cold, but it tasted great.

She looked at her notes and carefully followed the next step. *Plug the IP address into the search engine on the yougettool website.* Emily entered yougettool.com into the URL field and was quickly directed to a site with a picture of a world map and a search box. She copied and pasted the IP address into the search field and waited. Black arrows started to populate the screen, and Emily felt that she was watching a connect-the-dots contest. Thirty seconds passed, and the map was covered in lines and numbers. It took Emily a second to figure out what it all meant, but she soon realized that Prague was represented by the number 1—that made sense because she was now located in Prague and the message had been sent to her—while the sender's location was represented by the number 14. Wow. That message had traveled through fourteen different points around the world to reach her in Prague. She had always thought of e-mail as traveling in a straight line, and now here was a visual representation of the actual truth. Messages were more like balls ricocheting across the world, bouncing around from one point to the next.

Trying not to allow herself to get distracted by the details of those fourteen points, Emily focused on the final number, 14. She zoomed in to the page. She wanted a closer look at the location. Wait. Could she have made a mistake? It appeared that the sender's message had come from Madison, Wisconsin.

Twenty-One

Emily was about to do a Facebook search by copying the e-mail address into a search field and didn't notice that Pavel had come into her room. When he reached out to touch her arm, she yelped. Her nerves were threatening to burst from her skin—the events of the past several days had worked their cumulative stress magic on her. She was jangled.

Pavel shared highlights from his workday with her. He had gotten a job as a grade-school art teacher six months before. Emily could see bits of paint on his shirt and—was that glue on his pants? She smiled as he talked about his youngest pupil—a boy of five who loved to cut odd shapes of colorful paper and then glue or tape them to his own clothes. Most days Pavel had to hide the glue and tape from him, or the child's mother would invariably drag Pavel to the headmaster for berating. He told Emily he would've let the kid experiment with glue and fabric if it were his child, especially because the kid had an entire life of rules and order ahead of him, but it was unfortunately not his choice. "Just think where Picasso or Van Gogh would have ended up if they had never gotten dirty!"

Emily laughed out loud at that and thought about her own grade-school art classes. She couldn't remember them very well and wondered now if that was because her teachers were so structured or uninspired … or maybe uninspiring? All Emily knew was that she wished she had had Pavel as an art teacher. She would surely be reminiscing her early art days now instead of trying to recreate nonexistent memories.

They chose to eat at the restaurant Lokal for lunch. Emily had been there two years before and wanted to have the schnitzel with potato salad again. It was one of those flavorful dishes that could elicit savory memories years later. And she was definitely going to need an extra-large glass of Pilsner Urquell. It had been a very long day filled with lots of unexpected twists and turns, some pleasant and some, well … unexpected.

She had forgotten the interior of Lokal. Long wooden tables lined one side of the room while, on the other, huge, cold stainless steel tanks of beer stood waiting. Emily was sure they had been waiting for her for the past two years, and she was happy to be back. The beer was crisp and cold—just as she remembered it—and the food was simple yet delicious. Pavel ordered sausages with creamed horseradish and mustard while Emily settled on the schnitzel. As usual, the place was filled with locals and buzzing like a beehive. They had to sit with their heads close together if they wanted to hear each other. Emily felt as if she was shouting, but then again, everyone else was too.

They finished their meals and decided to stay for a couple more beers. It wasn't every day that Emily could boast having a drink in a local pub in Prague, and she wanted to soak in the atmosphere. She didn't have much time left in Prague and wanted to spend it wisely. She knew she still wanted to visit Terezin, the camp where Anna had been held, and she needed to talk to Bachmann at least one more time, at the very least by phone. If he had another lead or two on who could have known about Anna's music and stashed it away for safekeeping, then she would add that name to the list of people to visit as well. There was a chance they weren't even alive anymore, and even if they were, they might not be in Prague. But she would cross that bridge when she got to it.

She asked Pavel if he had time to drive her to Terezin in the morning. She had been there two years before, but she wanted to put herself in that setting one more time.

Pavel leaned across the table and shouted to Emily, "I can take you wherever you'd like. I took the day off tomorrow, so I'm all yours."

Emily was having trouble hearing Pavel. More people had crowded into the restaurant, and the high ceilings and stark furnishings made the sound ricochet off the walls. She would need to move closer. She got up and sat closer to Pavel so they could carry on a conversation. She felt lucky to have him as a friend. Who else would take the day off to drive her to a concentration camp? It wasn't exactly a place most people wanted to visit, and he had also driven her there the last time. She gave his hand a soft squeeze and told him how much she appreciated his help; it meant so much to her.

Pavel was so close now that when he spoke to her, his lips brushed her ear. She felt a tingle run down her neck and pulled away a bit. He didn't seem to notice but appeared to think she hadn't heard him, so he repeated what he had said. "Emily, I care about you."

She felt the familiar tingle again. She wasn't sure how to respond, but when she turned to him, their lips touched. Emily was about to pull away but felt herself drawn in instead. Then they were kissing. Pavel's hand went behind her head, and she felt her own hands reaching up to cup his face.

A voice interrupted them. "You two want another beer, or are you just about done?" The waitress was waiting with her small notepad. Emily turned and looked past her to the entryway of the restaurant. A long line had formed, and people were waiting for tables to open up. Emily turned to Pavel and said, "I think we'd better give some other people a chance to eat here. Let's pack it up and go."

On the metro ride back to Pavel's apartment, they both remained quiet. The clicking of the tracks and the repetitious movement of the train starting and stopping, doors opening and closing, lulled Emily into quiet reflection. She found herself mentally reviewing what had just happened. Had they really just kissed?

Pavel motioned to Emily that it was time to exit, and she reluctantly got up and left the train. She really wanted more quiet time to process what was going on. The last thing she wanted right now was to talk with Pavel about this. She didn't know herself how she felt about the kiss; how would she be able to talk to him?

She needn't have worried. As they walked the remaining four blocks to Pavel's apartment, he seemed as uninterested as she in revisiting what had just happened. Maybe they really could just act as though it had never happened?

* * *

Twenty-Two

Emily found herself unable to sleep; she could feel the warmth of Pavel's lips on hers each time she closed her eyes. She finally decided to give up trying to sleep and went to her computer. She flipped open her laptop and waited for it to warm up. If she couldn't sleep anyway, she may as well see what Szongas had to say to her. She couldn't run from her tenure-review results forever. And she had to admit, she was also curious to get back to her research on the identity of farandwide44.

She clicked on Szongas's message and waited for it to load. Ten seconds passed, then twenty … She reached into her suitcase and dug around for her cigarettes. She had packed them for emergencies only, but between the kiss and the anticipation of reading Szongas's message, she thought this moment qualified. She lit up a cigarette and watched as the message loaded.

> The tenure committee has unanimously agreed to grant Assistant Professor Emily Thurgood the status of Full Professor, effective January 2015. Prior to being awarded tenure in the Department of Musicology, however, Assistant Professor Thurgood will agree to fulfill the following requirements:
>
> - to serve as department chair for two consecutive years and then again every other year as part of a rotating cycle;
> - to publish at least four professional journal articles per year;

- to teach three courses per semester in the Department of Music;
- to act as primary consultant for external evaluation committees;
- to take on five additional doctoral dissertation candidates per year.

Emily drew on her cigarette slowly and then released the smoke even slower. On the one hand, this was most definitely a positive piece of news. To be awarded tenure was definitely better than to be denied tenure, but on the other hand, the list of requirements was an almost-unmanageable burden. How would she find time to conduct quality research if she had so many obligations? And what about her teaching? How would she be able to teach effectively if she were spreading herself so thinly? And what about her free time? And her private relationships?

The long list of conditions posed a catch-22 for Emily. She couldn't continue her work on music and the Holocaust without the full support of the university and funding from grants, but she also doubted her work would be as thorough as it had been if she had to divide her energies between committee work, teaching, writing, and advising. It occurred to her at that moment that her life at the university was going to change radically once she returned. She would have far less free time, where she already had precious little, and her personal relationships might suffer even more than they already had. She then thought about Brian and decided to call him with her news.

Emily dialed Brian's number and waited for him to pick up. The phone rang once, twice, three times. She assumed Brian had picked up because the ringing suddenly stopped. She spoke quickly before he could answer, "Guess what, Bri! I have some good news!"

A woman's voice responded, "I'm sorry, but Brian is in the shower. This is his girlfriend. Would you like to leave a message?"

The phone fell from Emily's hand.

It was then that Emily noticed that her cigarette had burned down to a mere stub, and she realized with a shock that the ashes had fallen onto Pavel's floor. She had to find a broom and dustpan to clean this up.

What kind of guest was she being if she left ashes and cigarette butts all over the place?

She got up to head for the cleaning closet just to find Pavel pacing in the hallway. His hair was tousled; he had clearly been running his hands through it repeatedly.

She nervously explained that she had accidentally dropped ashes on his floor and wanted to clean it up.

He stopped pacing to walk up to her. "You couldn't sleep either?"

Emily admitted she had been driven from the bed and decided to read her e-mail.

"Good news, I hope?" It was clear to Emily that Pavel was trying his best to make small talk, but his eyes revealed that his thoughts were somewhere else.

"Actually ..." Emily realized that she really wanted to confide in Pavel, so she asked if they could chat. She then shared the content of Szongas's message with him and told him how much it worried her that she might not be able to do the same quality of research if she had to work all the time. She then found herself telling Pavel about her phone call to Brian.

Pavel took her hands into his own. She tried to weigh her words carefully, but they sounded shallow to her ears. "Pavel, I care for you very much, but I am still involved with someone. I really don't know yet what that phone call meant." She was finding it hard to look him in the eye. She tried to keep her voice light. "Different time, different place perhaps."

His hands felt so warm in hers. He pulled her closer and took her face in his hands and said, "I think we both know what that phone call meant. And this is a different place. This is a different time." She realized then that her relationship with Brian had just come to an end.

* * *

TWENTY-THREE

While showering the next morning, Emily thought about what had happened. She needed to talk to Brian as soon as possible. This was not a conversation to have over the phone and absolutely not one to have over e-mail. If she were perfectly honest with herself, their relationship had always had its flaws. Brian was often impatient and frustrated by her erratic schedule, and she was often annoyed by his pedantic regularity and predictability. But then again, she thought, it was precisely the fact that she could depend on him that made her feel so safe. *Why is it,* she thought, *that the negative is so often also the positive?* Besides, he had been so helpful with her computer questions, and she liked to think that he appreciated her in many ways as well—despite her manic schedule and unpredictability. And, she reflected, which relationship didn't have flaws? But who was that woman who claimed to be Brian's girlfriend? How long had that been going on?

She then thought about Pavel and the previous evening. Jumping from the frying pan into the fire was definitely not a good idea. Maybe she was only attracted to Pavel because he offered her consolation after the strange phone call. And he was definitely an escape from her "real life." But if she was honest, she knew in her heart that she had always had feelings for him. She leaned back and let the water flow over her hair and face. God, why was everything always so complicated?

Just then Emily heard a muffled knock on the bathroom door and reached over to turn off the water. "Yes?" she yelled out.

"Just wondering if you want to leave any water for the rest of the Prague residents?"

Today was their day to visit Terezin. Emily sat on a small stool in front of the bathroom mirror and prepared herself for the trip. She reached for the hairbrush, and as she worked through the tangles of her long curls, Emily thought about the day that lay ahead. Though she had been to Terezin before, she wanted a fresh look at it. The last time she had been at Terezin, she had been mostly interested in general impressions; now she wanted to get a feeling for how the prisoners had lived and what the conditions at the camp were like. She also wanted to revisit the layout of the buildings, including the music hall, so she could contextualize how and where the musicians had performed and written music. Back then she had been looking for a general atmosphere; this time she was primarily interested in looking for clues about Anna. If she could find out what barracks Anna had been in, perhaps she could find a list of other women who had shared that space with her. Maybe one of them had helped to protect her music. Emily made a mental note to call Bachmann before they left to see if he had remembered anything else about who may have helped Anna hide her music.

Emily thought that another possibility was that Anna had actually hidden her music somewhere in the camp. She was hoping to get a sense of where Anna may have stashed sheets of music—in an attic, perhaps, or in a hole in a wall or maybe even under the floorboards? It was improbable that there was anything concrete left to be found in those places, but maybe she could at least get a sense for where Anna may have hidden her music. Emily remembered that some of the buildings had attics with nooks and crannies for stashing paper. She knew that some of the artists in the camp had hidden their drawings in the walls, and the elder Bachmann had just recently told her of the man who had hidden an entire diary from his time at Terezin in one of the attics there. Emily thought about the daily life stressors at the camp. Many of the prisoners at the camp were also in charge of running the day-to-day operations at the camp. It was hard enough for Emily to imagine the stress of living in captivity; she could not fathom how challenging it must have been to help run the camp as a prisoner. They would have had to become part of the machinery that held them. Some of the prisoners were doctors in the camp while some acted as Rabbi, cook, or even, in the case of Redlich, youth director. The stress of having to survive with extremely limited supplies and food and limited mobility while also being in charge of someone else's fate was unimaginable.

Just as Pavel announced that he was ready to take off, the phone rang. It was Bachmann, and he wanted to speak with Emily. She set the brush down and went to take the call.

Bachmann told her he had been unable to sleep and had ended up going through that same unbound collection of pictures and documents again. He had carefully reviewed all the old photographs that friends and family had sent him over the years. Many of them had been taken from the Internet—Bachmann mentioned how he still wasn't used to the ease with which information could be located and gathered.

Emily listened eagerly and waited for new news from her friend.

There was a long pause before he continued. "I noticed something, Emily."

Emily waited. "Bachmann, are you there?"

The air filled with his silence, and then he spoke slowly. "I'm fairly certain that Anna had a connection, a friend there, who wasn't one of us."

Emily asked him what this meant. Bachmann explained that Anna had studied music at the conservatory in Prague and that one of her music teachers there had also been at the camp—but not as a prisoner. He couldn't remember the name, and he didn't know if it was useful information, but he wanted to pass it on to her before he forgot.

"I am very grateful for your call and that information. I am certain it will be useful. Bachmann?"

"Yes?"

"We are going to Terezin now. Is there anything else you can think of that might be useful there?"

Silence filled the air.

"Bachmann? Are you still there?"

He spoke slowly, his voice sounding as if it had suddenly aged. "No. No, there is nothing useful there."

The trip north to Terezin would take an hour by car. As they drove, a light rain began to fall, and the sky slowly darkened from a light to a dark coal gray. The sun and then the sky gradually disappeared under the shadowy blanket. Emily reached over to adjust the heat settings on the dashboard, but Pavel told her it wouldn't do much good. The car heater hadn't worked in months. Emily pulled her thin jacket closer around her and gazed out the window. She hadn't slept well and was quickly lulled by the rain tapping softly on the window. Tap, tap, tap, and then a sudden rush of rain as the weather darkened. The wipers moved back and forth and acted as the accompaniment to the rhythm of the drops against the window. Whish, shwomp, whish, shwomp, whish, shwomp … Emily dozed and drifted to that place between wakefulness and sleep where what was real and what was imagined blended into a misty field. A skeleton tapped steadily on the windows with the thin bones of its fingers. Tap, tap, tap …

Pavel shook Emily awake. "Hey, we're here. The tour starts in ten minutes, so let's get a move on."

Emily blinked a few times. Her lids were heavy against her eyes, and it took effort to keep them open. Her arms pulled down at her sides, and it took strength to lift them up. Pavel was already opening the door on her side of the car before she was fully awake. The rain had slowed, but Pavel still held an umbrella up over the door so she wouldn't get wet when she got out of the car. She reached for his arm, and he pulled her from the car. Her dream state lingered momentarily, hanging on to the hope of pulling her back in.

By the time they reached the gates to Terezin, Emily had finally shaken herself free from the dream world. She stopped Pavel and pointed to the large letters at the top of the sign: *Arbeit macht frei.* Work sets you free. She shook her head and started to say something about the cruel irony of those words. Then she stopped and moved on. It was not necessary to tell Pavel what those harsh words meant. His own grandfather had been victim to those three powerful words and to the daily trials of the camp.

The Terezin Memorial allowed visitors to roam freely through the Small Fortress, the former barracks, and the ghetto museum. Emily wanted to concentrate on the barracks, as this was likely where Anna had spent most of her time. From the stories Bachmann had told her in his apartment, it didn't seem likely that she had been held in the Small Fortress, although it was impossible to guess whom the Nazis would have considered to be a political prisoner. There had been other structures used by the camp, but those had been turned over to Czech citizens after the war and were not part of the official memorial site. Emily had heard that it was possible to visit some of those private homes, but she was leaving Prague soon and was sure it would have taken too much time to organize a tour. She had to admit, though, that she would have been interested in one home in particular; it was said that the family that lived there had discovered a secret synagogue while they were cleaning. It gave Emily a shudder to think about the frightening consequences of secretly practicing a forbidden religion within the borders of a concentration camp.

Pavel and Emily walked slowly through the barracks. Emily ran her hand along the walls, trying to imagine the despair and fear the prisoners would have felt. She thought of the artists, writers, and composers who had hidden their sketches, stories, and music in the walls, and she tried to find a ridge or groove where that might have been possible. The walls were rough, but she couldn't see anything big enough to hide a sketch or any size paper for that matter. Hiding anything here had to have been virtually impossible. Pavel called to her to come over and look at something, and she made her way past the three-tier makeshift wooden bunks that had clearly been erected for the sole purpose of cramming more bodies into an already small space.

"What did you find?" she asked Pavel.

Pavel was pointing to a crack in the wall. "Look at this." It wasn't very large or very long, but Emily guessed the gap might have been big enough to stuff a piece of paper into it.

"Let's look for more like this." Emily moved more quickly now and closed her eyes as she ran her hand over the walls. It was ironically easier to "see" the cracks with her eyes closed. In a matter of minutes, she had found five or six possibilities for hiding paper—or even small objects. It was as if finding that first crack had made it possible to see the walls for the first time.

"What are you two doing in here?" The unfamiliar voice made Emily open her eyes. It was one of the official tour guides at the site. He was standing in the doorway, and Emily could see the name tag identifying him.

"We were just trying to imagine hiding something in the walls—uh, where the prisoners may have hidden things in the walls."

"So you know about that?" The guide moved closer.

Emily closed the gap between them and held out her hand. "My name is Emily Thurgood. I am visiting from the United States where I work as a music history professor. I have spent the past few years researching music in concentration camps."

He took Emily's hand and shook it warmly. "Moritz. Nice to be meeting you. I am working here for years, so I am knowing some stories. You are having questions?" He had a thick accent, but Emily was grateful he could speak some English.

Emily told him briefly about her mysterious piece of music, her attempt to discover the identity of the composer, and, finally, her discovery of Anna. She slowed down her speech when she saw the confusion on his face. "I'm sorry to trouble you, but do you think it would be possible to show me any lists with the prisoners' names? And maybe the years they were here as well?"

Moritz nodded and motioned for Emily to follow him. Emily looked to Pavel who took his place behind her.

Moritz led them to a special room and stood with them in front of a padlocked door. This chamber was not open to the general public, he explained, but was locked and protected and only opened when they received an official letter asking for permission to view special documents that had survived the war. He nodded to Emily and quietly said, "I see you need helping. It is my life mission to be helping people know about Terezin. Let us not worry about your lack of documents."

He told Emily about an electronic database that she could search if she wanted to find documents from that time, but he also told her it might be difficult to find exactly what she was looking for, especially if it hadn't been officially documented in the first place. The Nazis had been meticulous at documenting the individual names of prisoners who'd come into Terezin. They also had detailed lists of those who had been transported out of Terezin. But anything that might have been carried out secretly, such as "drawing pictures" or "writing stories" or music, could easily have gotten lost to time.

Emily was already aware of the database, but precisely as Moritz was suggesting, it had proven to be useless for her current purposes. She asked Moritz what was on the other side of the door.

"Ah," he said slowly. "There are some things in here reserved for special visitors. Of course you must first put on gloves please." He unlocked the door and let them into a dusty room. Emily could see three long tables covered with boxes. She looked at Moritz and pointed to the boxes. "May I?"

Moritz made a sweeping gesture. "Yes. This is what I want to show you. You are lucky we are having few visitors today. I am happy to share this with one such as yourself, who can make world know about this place."

She thanked Moritz for trusting her and asked Pavel to work from right to left while she started on the left side. They would meet in the middle—unless one of them found something useful before then.

Emily and Pavel both put on cotton gloves, and Emily reminded Pavel to handle the documents with extreme care; clearly little had been done to preserve the integrity of the sheets. Emily thought to herself what a shame that funding for their preservation did not seem to be a top priority.

She had already started carefully lifting papers from the first box when she heard Moritz quietly ask if there was anything he could do to help. She was touched by his offer and turned her head to tell him over her shoulder that they were looking for anything with the name Anna K. or Anna Katz. "She would have been here in 1942 sometime and may have been here even as late as 1944. We're not 100 percent sure about her dates here, but hopefully that information will help us."

Emily went back to examining the sheets one by one, careful not to harm the fragile papers in the process. *There really needs to be more funding somewhere for long-term preservation,* she thought. She was so focused on her work that she didn't even notice when Moritz did not respond; she only took in his strangely still stature when she was moving on to the second box of papers. It was then that she turned to him and saw that he was quietly crying.

"Moritz?" She took off her gloves and moved quickly to where he was standing in the middle of the room. "What is the matter? I'm so sorry. Have I said something to upset you?"

Moritz shook his head and, so quietly that Emily thought she hadn't heard correctly, said, "Anna Katz was my grandmother's sister. She never had her own children because of all of this." He waved a hand past the buildings in Terezin. "She was my great-aunt, but I did not meet her. I can tell you her dates. She died in Auschwitz on October 16, 1944."

* * *

Twenty-Four

Emily had heard many strange stories of coincidence: a baby, falling from a window two separate times, saved both times by the same man; twin brothers, although separated at birth, had both been named James, had both become police officers, and had both married women named Linda. She had often wondered at the veracity of these and other such stories and often thought of the expression "You can't make this stuff up." And now here she was, in a city halfway across the world from where she lived, coincidentally meeting the grandchild of the woman who had written the single sheet of music that had mysteriously been delivered to her by an unknown stranger. She thought again of the expression: "You can't make this stuff up."

Moritz's voice cut through her thoughts. "What is this meaning? Can't make stuff up?"

She realized she had said those words out loud and apologized to Moritz. She walked up to him and put her arms around him in a hug. She then said to him, "Thank you for being here today. I am so grateful."

Pavel joined them and asked Moritz if he had already been through all the boxes. Moritz nodded and told them he got off work in an hour. Perhaps they could go back to his apartment so he could show them what he had found on his own search?

Emily thought again about strange falling babies and separated twins. What bizarre twist of fate had brought them all together today?

During the hour that they waited for Moritz to finish his work, Emily and Pavel wandered around the Terezin Memorial grounds. The rain had turned into a fine, cold mist. It wasn't enough to warrant an umbrella, but Emily found herself pulling her hood up over her head. The temperature had also dropped, and her fingers and toes were beginning to stiffen in the cold.

She walked closer to Pavel, hooking her arm into his and putting her hand into his pocket for warmth. As they strolled, she could see that he was smiling. "Hey, what are you laughing about?" She poked him in the side through his pocket.

He turned and kissed the top of her head. "Just amazed by your luck is all."

It was true. She reflected on what she had accomplished on such a short visit to Prague: Bachmann's invaluable help identifying Anna, Moritz's almost miraculous appearance, and Pavel's unceasing support and friendship. Not to mention the deepening friendship with Bachmann and recent romantic developments with Pavel. How *had* she been so lucky? Could this really all be just a coincidence? She thought again about the falling baby and the twin boys and laughed.

Pavel wrapped his arm around her waist and looked at her. "What's so funny with you now?"

She leaned toward him and gave him a gentle kiss. "Nothing really. Just amazed by my luck."

Moritz was waiting for them at the gates to the camp. He gave them directions to his apartment and told them he'd meet them in twenty minutes. He just wanted to pick up some small things first.

On the way to Moritz's, they stopped at a small market and picked up some beer, a loaf of fresh bread, and some cheese. It was getting close to dinner, and they didn't want to impose on Moritz's hospitality. As they drove the short distance to his apartment, Emily took in their surroundings; wide, expansive fields opened up before them, and she could just barely make out rolling hills in the distance. They were on a rough country dirt road now—two lines of well-worn ground where wheels had rolled again and again, pounding what had once been grass into dirt. Emily squinted past the rain on her window and noticed that the road had no shoulder to boast of and merely dropped straight down into a ravine. She gasped as she realized how treacherous the driving had suddenly become. As the rain started to pick up again, Pavel turned his wipers on high. Fwack, fwack, fwack, fwack … The noise they were making was almost violent, and Emily's thoughts went back to the wartime conditions at the camp. She covered her ears and asked Pavel if he could slow them down. He leaned in toward the windshield, and Emily could see that he was having trouble seeing. "This road is very rough, Emily, and I'm afraid I'll run off the path if I turn down the wipers at all. Hopefully we're almost there."

Emily scolded herself for being so selfish. The noise really was grating on her nerves, but Pavel needed to see where he was going.

Emily tried to imagine what Moritz would have to show them. She was eager to learn more about Anna; Bachmann's descriptions had made it feel as if Anna was in the room with them. Maybe Moritz would even have some more clues about the sheet of music Bachmann had identified as Anna's.

Her thoughts suddenly drifted to Harold Hansen. As preoccupied as she had been with finding the identity of the mysterious composer whom she now knew to be Anna, she hadn't given Hansen or his murder a second thought lately. She realized with a pang of guilt that she had been more interested in finding out who had composed the music and had completely pushed away her real reason for making the trip to Prague: finding a possible connection between the sheet of music left on her desk and Harold Hansen's murder. What had those strange words meant: "Look to the music"? She wondered if and how everything was connected: Hansen's murder, Anna's music, the mysterious caller.

She thought back to Hansen's original midnight call to her office. He had wanted to show her something. Was whatever it was connected to Anna's music and to the caller?

She let her thoughts wander to the police and what they might have discovered since she had left Wisconsin for Prague. Perhaps they had found the killer. Or could they still believe she had something to do with his death?

"Emily? Emily? Are you about ready to go inside?" Pavel had stopped the car and now put his hand on her arm. He was shaking it gently, as if trying to wake her from a deep sleep.

Emily blinked a few times and shook away thoughts of Hansen. She nodded to Pavel, and they made their way to the door, where Moritz was waiting.

They started with a simple dinner; bread and butter, cheese, beer, some sliced meats, and a jar of pickles that Moritz had conjured up from the fridge. As they ate, Moritz told them about his great-aunt's life before the war. She had studied composition at the Prague Conservatory, he said. She played the piano exceptionally well and had made a fairly decent living as an accompanist—for the other music students at the conservatory as well as for the many other musicians in Prague. Moritz buttered another slice of bread and motioned for Emily to pass him the meat platter. Anna had been able to save quite a bit of money during those days; everyone at the conservatory needed an accompanist at one point or another—for recitals, competitions, juries. Anna had never been short of work.

They finished their meal and took their beers to the living room, where Moritz pulled out an album of family pictures. He slowly flipped through the pages until he found one of Anna at the piano. Her hands were lovely, Emily thought—long, delicate fingers that held secret magic. Her hair was swept up and back off her face in a grandiose pompadour style, and she was wearing fiery-red Bohemian garnet earrings and a matching necklace. Emily remembered hearing once that Bohemian garnet was also a spiritual stone: it was meant to help drive away sorrow and bring the wearer a sense of joy and happiness. Anna's black floor-length gown shimmered even now off the black-and-white page. Emily mentioned to Moritz that the picture reminded her of Hedy Lamarr—the famously elegant Austrian American actress.

Moritz nodded. "Yes, she was very dark like that. Beautiful too, but not just in looks. Her spirit was strong," He paused. "And she was so kind."

Emily asked if Moritz had other pictures of Anna. He turned the pages of the album slowly, stopping once and again to look at the family pictures with what Emily thought might have been a yearning for things gone by. He settled on a picture on the last page of the book, and Emily thought it was likely the last one of Anna in the collection. He passed the book to Emily and Pavel so they could look more closely. Emily could feel Pavel's breath on her hair as they sat together over the album. Anna was sitting on a bench. She appeared to be all alone, and there was a small suitcase on the floor to her right. She was wearing a heavy woolen coat and thick gloves. Emily thought her face looked hopeful. Emily turned to Moritz and asked, "Was she going on a trip in this picture?"

Moritz nodded slowly. "She certainly thought so. Life had become very difficult for all of them, and Anna had heard there was a better place for people like us. She even paid money to go there, but she never returned." They unfortunately understood what he meant.

* * *

TWENTY-FIVE

June 23, 1944

Pani Svobodova had snuck away to bring Anna some dried meat and to take Anna's last sheets of music. "Today we will have an important visit from the International Red Cross. They are here to see how beautiful our camp is and what a nice life you all have," she explained. "I need to take your music for safekeeping. I will do my best to keep you safe through the end of this." Svobodova took the music from Anna, folded the sheets of music in half, and stuffed them into her shirt. "I will protect these pages. Don't worry. But, Anna, I must tell you I cannot help you anymore. It is too dangerous. Good luck."

Officials at the camp called the choir together to prepare a concert of Verdi's Requiem for the International Red Cross. Anna stood by the window of the music building and looked out. She could see different groups being forcibly formed and police guards ordering people around. Kindergarten children were called to sing songs. Another woman in the choir joined Anna and told her that she had heard that plays and other performances were being organized and that the prisoners would have to play sports for the International Red Cross visit. Anna's stomach churned as she watched two prisoners erect a sign for the "School for Boys and Girls" on a building that had been forcibly vacated. She could see that the sign also read "Currently on Vacation." A guard stood nearby and watched. She saw other guards ordering prisoners to haul benches into the "school."

In the music room there were whispers of what was happening. Many members of the choir were nervous about performing because so many members had been lost to disease and deportation.

* * *

TWENTY-SIX

January 2014

Emily carefully closed the album and asked Moritz if he had any other documents or papers of Anna's from before or during the war. He announced that he first needed a hot drink and went into the kitchen, returning a few minutes later with small cups of steaming hot coffee. Emily cupped her hands around the tiny cup and listened quietly while Moritz talked about Anna's compositions.

"She wrote about fifteen pieces before the war; some of those were for solo piano, but most were for mixed ensembles. She had a remarkable sense of harmony and rhythm and was very ..." He paused as he searched the air with his hand for the correct word. "... analyzing?"

Emily filled in the blank for him. "Analytical."

Moritz nodded gratefully and told them how Anna typically worked. She would create an outline on paper—much as a writer would do before starting a large project like a novel—and then she would work from there, developing themes and subthemes and embellishing variations as she went along. Her work was rarely derivational, but she drew her inspiration from politics and society. It wasn't unusual, he explained, for Anna to turn to literature, specifically poetry, to inspire her to write music.

Emily asked him to elaborate. He stood up and motioned for them to join him in the next room. There was a small piano in the corner; Emily briefly wondered how common it was for Czech houses to have pianos. Moritz asked Pavel and Emily to sit on a small sofa not far from the instrument, and he thumbed through a box of papers until he found the one he was looking for. He set it up on the piano and began to play. The piece started quietly. A repetition of simple minor-chord progressions repeating in the left hand only: I–IV–I–IV–I. Emily thought it sounded like the key of d minor. She closed her eyes and imagined herself marching quietly but somberly through a dark forest.

The right hand gradually joined in on an upbeat. High notes. Trills repeated on the upbeat. Emily could see clouds clearing and heard birds in the forest, following her as she walked down a snowy path. Both hands started moving swiftly across the keys now. Water rushing down a stream. Emily continued down the path and noticed snow roses—that persistent flower that blossoms through snow. She could hear the right hand delicately dancing across the keys while the left returned to a quiet march.

There was an inherent sadness to the music but also a hopeful, wistful quality. It reminded Emily of the photograph of Anna sitting on the bench. Perhaps deep down she had somehow suspected what would come next for her? She had been yearning for a better life, but maybe on some level she also had known that where she was going was anything but a paradise.

Moritz ended the piece and stared at the keyboard. He sat like that for several seconds before turning to Emily and Pavel. "I haven't played that music in years. My great-aunt wrote that before the war. It is called 'The Forest.'"

Emily opened her eyes and told Moritz that she had imagined walking through the woods the entire time he had been playing. He nodded. "Yes, she intended to evoke that sensation in the listener, but she also used key elements from a popular workers' song from the time."

She asked him what he meant by that. "She commonly took letters from words and interpreted them musically."

Pavel asked how it was possible to write words with musical notes. Emily explained that it was a technique that actually had a long tradition. She stood and went to the piano and asked Moritz if she could play something. He made way for her on the bench, and she played four single notes: B-flat, A, C, B-natural. They she turned to both men and asked them if they recognized what she had just played. Moritz smiled and nodded, but Pavel shook his head.

Emily played the sequence again. "That's Bach's name. The German system for note naming is different from the English one: the note B-flat represents the letter *B*, the notes A and C clearly stand for the letters *A* and *C*, and the note B-natural represents *H.* Bach often used these four notes in his music as a way of signing a piece as his own. In other words, he buried, or hid, the letters from his name in the music itself." She went on to say that Brahms had done something similar with his family name in the A-flat minor organ fugue with the notes B-flat, A, B-natural, and E-flat all representing letters from his family name. Schumann had hidden romantic messages in his music *Carnaval* to his romantic interest Ernestine von Fricken, and even Alban Berg, a student of Arnold Schoenberg, had hidden dissonant messages of his own in pieces like the *Lyric Suite*.

As she spoke about the history of musical cryptograms, Emily was reminded of her recent meeting with Bachmann. He had pointed out similar messages in Anna's music: *Gebt den Glauben nicht auf!* Don't give up believing! Anna had hidden key letters from that phrase in the sheet that Emily had found in her office: the notes G, D, B, and A were all strategically placed to deliver a message.

Here was one more piece of evidence that the music she had found in her office had likely also been composed by Anna. The cryptographic pattern was similar; hiding words and letters in her music was something akin to Anna's signature. Emily asked Moritz if he had any other examples of Anna's work. She placed her hand on his arm and quietly asked, "Perhaps from her time at Terezin?"

Moritz shook his head. "Sadly, I found nothing from there."

* * *

Twenty-Seven

October 16, 1944

The choir was to perform Verdi's Requiem for the sixteenth time. Anna was tired, and her muscles ached all over, but she knew Verdi's music would lift her spirits. There were only sixty singers left in the choir, and Anna wondered how powerful the music would be with only sixty weak and tired singers. She thought back to Schächter's words: "We will sing to them what we cannot say to them."

The singers stood together and sang Verdi. Collaboratively, as one single choir. Anna could feel the spirituality flowing through her as they worked through the many movements to the final words of Verdi's libretto, "Libera me" ("Liberate me"). As they finished the piece, Anna's mind wandered to open fields of flowers, family holidays, tables full of hot, steaming food, and for a moment, she felt free too.

When the concert ended, a guard came into the room and told them that most of them would be on the next transport east. He announced to everyone that it was time to take a train ride. Anna thought she was still dreaming, but then a rough hand was yanking on her arm. "You. Now. Move."

Before she had time to register what was happening, Anna was in line with half of the women in her barracks, walking silently toward the train. As the sun went down on the horizon, darkness began to fall in Terezin. They were marched past the row of trees that had been planted just a few months before. Anna looked around herself to take in who was in line with her to the train. Almost the entire choir. The women, the men … and there was Schächter out in front.

He turned just then, and she caught his glance and held it. She could see him mouthing the very last words of Verdi's libretto: "Libera me." She nodded and continued walking toward the train.

* * *

Twenty-Eight

January 2014

By the time Pavel and Emily got back to Pavel's apartment, it was late. Emily quickly packed her small bag and the few souvenirs she had bought over the past few days. She hadn't wanted to risk breaking the delicate porcelain of Blue Onion–patterned dishes or delicate crystal glassware, so she'd decided to buy her colleague Mark a Dvorak CD and the sheet music for Dvorak's *Slavonic Dances* for two pianos. For Natalia she'd bought *The Unbearable Lightness of Being* by Czech author Milan Kundera, and Brian would get some postcards and an original Budvar beer. She had been stuck on what to get him; the uncertainty of what awaited them made it difficult to choose a gift carefully. A bottle of beer seemed safe enough.

For herself, she chose a pair of delicate Bohemian garnet earrings. They were a bit of a splurge, but she thought she might need some help with future sorrow.

Right before her flight took off, Emily got a text from Brian that he had an unexpectedly full schedule and wouldn't be able to make it to the airport in Chicago. He suggested that they meet in a few days; he said he wanted to talk to her about something important.

Emily could guess what that important thing was—or better *who* it was. All the signs were pointing to an imminent breakup, and as much as she felt it was probably for the best, she was still dreading that conversation. She was terrible at ending things and had to admit she was not quite ready for that talk. She was relieved he wasn't able to pick her up. She quickly texted Mark and asked if he could get her instead; she wanted to talk with him about the last several days anyway.

The flight back to Chicago passed more quickly than her first flight to Prague, primarily because the seat behind her was empty, and she was actually able to spend part of the flight sleeping. She dreamed about Anna dancing the waltz in her long black dress, and Emily could see the flash of her brilliant garnet earrings whenever she would spin around. Her dancing partner looked strangely familiar.

Mark loved his CD recording and the sheet music for Dvorak's *Slavonic Dances* for two pianos. He and Emily would often play four-hand pieces together, so it was a great addition to his collection.

As they drove, Emily got Mark caught up on the past several days. He wasn't surprised by Szongas's e-mail and news of her tenure or her increased workload; there had been rumors circulating that the department, like many other humanities programs all over the country, was in trouble and was needing to double-duty its newly tenured faculty. Instead of hiring more professors, the inner group of older, tenured professors had decided to have fewer hands do more of the work. Mark said it was nothing personal; it was happening all over in higher education—very few departments were being spared from economic hardship. Even the well-established and wealthier law schools were feeling the crunch.

Emily still wasn't so sure it wasn't a personal vendetta against her, but as she had no concrete proof, she kept quiet. She also decided to withhold recent romantic developments with Pavel from Mark for the time being. She wasn't sure herself what was going to happen with that one—why poke the bear unnecessarily?

Mark glanced over at Emily briefly while he drove and asked her if she had discovered anything interesting about the page of music someone had left for her. She wasn't sure why, but she hesitated telling him everything. She glossed over the details of hidden messages and musical subterfuge and stuck to Bachmann's general discovery that it was likely Anna Katz who had composed the music.

Mark looked over at Emily again; she hated it when people did that while driving and really wished he'd keep his eyes on the road. "Anna Katz? Don't think I've heard that name before."

Emily then told Mark that Anna had been at Terezin—probably sometime around 1942—and had managed, as far as she could tell, to continue composing music during her internment.

The car was starting to veer toward the middle line in the road, and Emily made a small yelping noise. Mark jerked the wheel to the right to adjust the path of the car and asked Emily for more information. "And your friend thinks she wrote that piece while she was at Terezin?"

Emily nodded and then realized Mark might look over at her again, so she put words to her gestures: "Yes. He knew her while she was there."

This time the car started swerving to the right, and Emily wondered briefly if Mark may have been drinking. It was only noon, but maybe he had had some wine with lunch? Or perhaps he was preoccupied with something. She offered to take over driving.

"No, no, sorry. I am just a bit tired is all. I've had some late nights trying to get my own tenure portfolio ready."

The discussion then moved back to Szongas's e-mail announcing that Emily had received tenure and the long list of conditions for her continued employment. Emily's voice turned dark as she muttered under her breath, "I still think the son of a bitch hates women."

Mark shook his head. "You are most decidedly paranoid, Em. If Szongas was a full-blown misogynist, you likely wouldn't have gotten tenure at all."

She had to grant him that point, especially when he pointed out the pattern with recent tenure reviews in the department. She learned as they talked that, out of four candidates total, she had been the only one to have been awarded tenure recently. She had to admit then that she had been too preoccupied with preparing her own portfolio and trying to keep herself free of suspicion from the police to follow the other tenure reviews very closely. She hadn't even realized three other candidates had failed the review process. They were in slightly different areas from Emily—two were in performance music, organ and piano, and the other was in the jazz department. It occurred to her then that she no longer knew what was going on with the Hansen case either. She had been far removed from local news developments and had no idea what the updates were. She asked Mark to fill her in.

"Well, interestingly, now the police seem preoccupied with the ex-wife. They think that she may have had something to gain from killing him—I heard some vague thing about an insurance policy or something similar, and they have been holding her for questioning." Mark looked over at Emily again, and the car started pulling slightly to the right. Emily wondered if Brian had had anything to do with steering the police in Gloria's direction and made a mental note to talk to Brian about what he knew. She also decided to stop distracting Mark for the rest of the ride home and quit talking.

By the time Emily got home, she could feel jet lag setting in. She made herself a cup of Earl Grey tea, and as the tea bag steeped, she turned on her computer. As tired as she was, she knew she wouldn't be able to sleep, so she decided to check on something. She scrolled through her e-mail messages until she found what she was looking for. There it was: farandwide44. She read through the message again. "Have you found any answers? Keep looking to the music, and you will find your way." Answers. Look to the music. Find your way. She thought about what she now knew. She knew that this message had originated in Madison. She knew that Anna had composed the music left in her office. But she didn't know much more than that.

She wondered if the e-mail message was from someone she knew personally. As she went through the events of the last two weeks, she began subconsciously tapping a rhythm on the table, and after a few beats, she started humming a melody. In her mind, she heard a piano playing. What was it she had thought that first time she had heard that piece? It was a "haunting melody" with "piercingly lonely" harmonies … At that moment, Emily knew she had to talk to Henry Cramer. He had shown such an interest in Emily's work. Could he help her solve this musical mystery?

She called Mark to get Cramer's telephone number. For some reason, she didn't have it in her directory. Mark immediately asked why she needed it and then teased her that she just wanted to pick up where they had left off.

She snapped at him, "What the hell is that supposed to mean?"

He laughed and said, "Methinks the lady doth protest too much. You're awfully snappy, Emily. What should I think it means when you call for his number?" Then he told her that he wasn't the only one who had noticed how chummy they had seemed during Cramer's visit. He asked if anything had happened between them.

She was not in the mood for this. "Mark, could you please just give me the number? I can't seem to find it, and I need to speak with him about something."

"Well, if you don't need it to make a date with him, then what do you need it for?"

"None of your business."

With that, he hung up. The jet lag was making her cranky. She would call back and apologize in a minute for being so short with him, but first she wanted to see if she could find Cramer's number or maybe his e-mail address another way.

She did a simple search of her e-mail messages and was able to find Cramer's e-mail address fairly quickly. She would have preferred calling him, but this would have to do for now. She didn't have the energy for a drawn-out apology with Mark. She was acting on a hunch, and Mark would want details she didn't have. She dashed off a quick message to Cramer that she needed to speak with him and then logged off her account. Now she would just have to wait for his call.

* * *

Twenty-Nine

Twenty minutes later she was snuggled in a warm bed, ready to give in to the jet lag; the ringing of the doorbell jolted her out of her half-sleep state, and she groggily made her way to the front door. It was Mark. He was holding a small bouquet of flowers.

"Sorry about before. I shouldn't have hung up on you." He handed her the flowers and asked if he could come in.

Emily was bone-tired and not in the mood for a serious talk, but she sensed it couldn't wait. She motioned to the couch and asked Mark if he wanted some tea. As long as she was up, she might as well have another cup.

They sat together on the plush sofa, and Emily had to fight off the sleep that was threatening to descend.

"Emily, I haven't been completely honest with you." Mark was sitting on the edge of the sofa; Emily forced herself to sit up straight.

"What do you mean? Honest about what?" She cupped the hot tea in her hands. Her thoughts were drifting to her warm bed.

Mark then told her that he had known Cramer a very long time. They had gone to the same music school together a few years earlier. Emily thought he was being strangely sensitive about such an innocuous piece of information and told him so.

"That's not exactly what I haven't been honest about." Mark seemed to be waiting for her to read his mind. "I need to tell you something about Cramer."

"Just tell me what's on your mind already. I'm cranky and tired." Emily took a sip of tea and waited.

Mark then told her that he hadn't seen Cramer in several years but had run into him a year before at a music conference in San Antonio.

They had spent some time in the hotel bar talking about old times. One thing had led to another, and Cramer had admitted that he was feeling depressed; he was stuck in a rut and felt he had nowhere to go. His compositions felt uninspired, and music was not fulfilling him the way he had always hoped it would. Mark had shared with Cramer his own fears about tenure and job security.

Perhaps he had had one glass of wine too many, but Mark then had decided to tell Cramer about a research trip to Germany that he had taken the year before. During that trip, Mark had unexpectedly found a music manuscript that had seemed important somehow; he didn't know who had composed the piece because there was no clear marking on it, but the harmonies and melodies had floated off the page at him. Mark had told Cramer he'd decided on the spur of the moment to take the manuscript with him so he could analyze it later. No one had even noticed when he'd slipped the manuscript into his bag and walked out of the archive with it. He had never actually intended to keep it.

Emily sat up and interrupted Mark's story. "What exactly are you saying, Mark? Are you seriously telling me that you stole a manuscript from an archive? Please tell me you did not just say that."

Mark looked down at his hands and nodded. "Yes, Em. I am sorry to say that I did. I still don't know what got into me that day. In my defense, I was starting to panic about job security and was very worried about losing my job. I guess I hoped that a major new discovery might help me out of my predicament, and I just wanted some time to analyze the piece on my own. I really never intended things to get out of control the way that they did."

Emily thought there were other ways to protect yourself against job loss, but she decided to keep it to herself and asked Mark to continue. "What exactly do you mean by 'out of control'?"

Mark took a moment to look Emily in the eye and told her he wasn't proud of his actions but that she needed to listen to the whole story. Her life could depend on it.

He continued quietly, "I will forever regret that night, and I honestly believe that if I hadn't had that last drink, I might never have mentioned taking the manuscript to this man who I considered to be a friend."

Emily found herself thinking this was not the time to blame such a big mistake on a glass of wine, but she bit her tongue. She was wide awake now and asked Mark to explain what he meant.

"Emily, I swear I never meant for things to work out this way. They took on a dynamic of their own." He explained that Cramer had convinced him to meet him in Chicago a week later, so he could see the music. He'd told Mark he simply wanted to judge for himself if the piece was significant. Mark had convinced himself that Cramer was just trying to help Mark analyze the piece.

Mark explained that he had been so concerned about his job security that he'd agreed—against his better judgment. But he'd also guessed he had already crossed a pretty significant line anyway when he had slipped the manuscript into his bag in the archive. What harm could it possibly do now to have another musicologist take a look at it?

Emily dreaded the next part of Mark's story.

"A week later, I met with Cramer. After spending time carefully analyzing the piece, Cramer offered to pay me fifty thousand dollars for the music in exchange for my complete discretion. Emily, I honestly thought he was joking and started putting the music back into my bag, but Cramer insisted he wasn't bluffing.

"Ten days after that, Cramer proved how serious he was when he wired the money into my account. I rationalized that no one would notice the missing manuscript anyway. What harm could it do? I delivered the music to Cramer—no questions asked."

Emily had a sinking feeling in her belly as Mark continued his story. "Two months later, at one of Cramer's composition concerts, I thought Cramer's newest composition sounded eerily familiar. With a pang of self-disgust, I realized it was the piece I had stolen and passed on to him. And Cramer was claiming that he himself had written it."

Emily felt a chill pass down her spine. The sonata. She had always known there was something different about Cramer's piano sonata. And she had thought it odd that Cramer didn't ever want to talk about that piece, even though it was clearly some of his best writing. *Correction,* Emily thought, *someone else's best writing.*

Emily tried to remain calm. She was afraid to ask but needed to know. "Well, what did you do then?"

Mark shrugged his shoulders. "What could I do? I had stolen a manuscript from an archive and sold it for fifty thousand dollars. If I had said anything, we both would have gone to jail. I kept my mouth shut and hoped everything would go away."

"But then?"

Mark looked away from Emily. "After that, I didn't hear from Cramer again until the phone call."

Emily felt a sense of dread. "Until what phone call?"

"The phone call where Cramer asked me if he could come to the university to perform. Mainly, though, he wanted to meet you." Emily felt Mark waiting for what he had said to sink in.

Emily wasn't sure she understood. "What is this all about? How am I connected to this whole thing?"

Mark said he didn't know. But he guessed her librarian had something to do with it.

"My librarian? Do you mean Hansen?"

Mark nodded. "I don't think it's a coincidence that Hansen was killed around the same time Cramer appeared."

Emily slowly asked him to explain what he meant by that.

"God, Emily, do I really need to spell it out? I think Cramer might have had something to do with Hansen's death. And I'm worried now that he thinks you might be on to him, and he might be after you next."

Emily felt as if there were fire ants on her neck. "Why on earth would he be after me?"

Mark shrugged. "I'm guessing Cramer's trying to see how much you know." He paused. "Let's just say I don't think it's wise for you to be contacting Cramer on your own. I'm coming with you when you see him next. Get a good night's sleep tonight, Emily."

* * *

THIRTY

Emily was still trying to put all the pieces together when the phone rang. It was Cramer. He told her he was thrilled to see her e-mail message in his box and that he had really missed her. She felt a shudder. He asked when they could meet, and Emily asked if she could meet him in the morning and if he would mind if she brought Mark.

There was a pause before Cramer answered, "I was really hoping you wanted to see me alone, Emily. I have to admit you're bruising my ego now." Emily had to bite her tongue to keep from blurting out what she knew.

It would take three hours to drive to him, so he offered to meet her in the middle. There was a truck stop halfway to Chicago where they could meet for coffee. He gave her directions and told her he'd be there at eleven o'clock. She forced herself to say how pleased she was that he could meet her so soon.

* * *

There was no way Emily was going to get to sleep now. She wondered what the connection was between her and Hansen—and Anna? She had an idea who might know something of use, and she dialed Gloria's number. If she was lucky, Gloria might be able to help her.

Emily apologized for called Gloria so late, but Gloria almost seemed to be expecting Emily's call. Emily didn't hesitate and asked Gloria if she was farandwide44. Gloria quietly admitted that she had been the one to send Emily the e-mail messages telling her to "look to the music."

"I don't understand. What does it mean?" Emily still wasn't connecting the dots between Hansen, Cramer, Anna and herself.

"That music I left on your desk?" Gloria waited to see that Emily was still there.

"Yes?"

"The signature is the same."

"What signature do you mean?"

"You know, the name on the page. Anna K. It's the same on both compositions. I don't know what it all means, but that Cramer person—you know, that composer who played at the university after Harold's death? Harold saw a copy of the original sheet music for his sonata. The signature is the same as the piece I put on your desk."

Emily couldn't speak. Anna K.? Her thoughts flew back to Prague, to Bachmann, to Pavel … and to Anna Katz. She had written the piano sonata that Cramer was claiming to have written himself. And how could Gloria have known all of this?

"Emily? Are you there? Emily?"

"Yes, Gloria, I'm still here. I'm just trying to get my head around all of this." Emily told Gloria everything then—how she had taken the trip to Prague to see Bachmann, what she had learned about Anna, how Anna had survived in the concentration camp by writing and playing music. She thought she might vomit as she then thought of Cramer paying Mark so much money for a piece of music that Anna had likely composed during the horrific time in Terezin. How Anna had died there. And, finally, how Cramer was now passing off Anna's composition as his own.

She asked Gloria where the music on her desk had come from.

"Harold gave it to me for safekeeping. He told me he wanted to meet with you, but when you couldn't meet with him right away, he contacted me and asked me to hang on to it. He thought he might be in danger."

Emily's mind was racing. "Gloria, why didn't you give it to me earlier? Why all the shadows and fog with farandwide44? Why were you hiding the truth from me all this time?" Emily was doing her best to piece everything together.

Gloria admitted it hadn't been the best way to handle everything, but she was worried about being sent to jail. She stood to inherit a lot of money after Harold's death, and the last thing she needed was to be caught in the middle of an international theft.

Emily still couldn't understand where Harold had gotten Anna's music. How or even if he had made the connection between Anna's music and Cramer. How he had thought Emily would be able to help. She asked Gloria what she knew.

"Harold told me the grandson of a Professor Svobodova sent him that music I ended up leaving on your desk. He was apparently aware that the manuscript was missing from the archive, and he knew that the real composer had been in a concentration camp. He knew Harold from some research Harold had done in the Czech Republic, and he wanted help in finding the person who had stolen something from his grandmother's friend. Harold was a big fan of your work on music during the Holocaust, and he thought you might be able to help him figure out the final puzzle piece."

Emily's heart sank as she realized what that meant. *Harold died in the process of bringing truth to light.*

As she slowly hung up the phone, Emily reflected on everything that had happened over the previous weeks—Harold's death, the pressing decision about tenure, the situation with Brian, and even recent developments with Pavel. Despite all the insecurities and unknowns in her own life, she now knew one thing for sure. Her next call was going to be to the police. She would do her best to make sure that Cramer became famous for something other than *his* new composition. He needed to pay for stealing Anna's music and taking credit for her genius.

* * *

THIRTY-ONE

A year later, once Emily was satisfied that Cramer would be tried and punished, she made a decision which surprised everyone who knew her. She turned down the tenure offer, packed her bags, and accepted a non-tenure-track teaching position at the Prague Conservatory.

She relied on the generosity of her many friends and contacts in Prague to get settled. Pavel had helped her find a small apartment in the center of the city, and she had quickly reestablished ties to the many musicians and families she had gotten to know during her research. She had even contacted Professor Svobodova's grandson and had learned that Anna Katz's music included more than the piano sonata which Cramer had illegally claimed as his own. Professor Svobodova had miraculously also managed to save several of Anna's other compositions, including a string quartet, two additional piano pieces, and a small collection of folk songs arranged for women's voices. Emily had not had a chance to analyze them all yet, but she had a hunch there was more to Anna's music than met the eye.

The elder Bachmann introduced Emily to a small group of individuals who occasionally organized concerts in Prague. When Emily suggested that they put on a concert of recently discovered music which had been written in Terezin, they eagerly agreed.

As the audience got settled and the lights dimmed, Emily's thoughts moved to Steinitz, Schächter, Anna, and all the countless others who had found a way to sing what they couldn't say. The pianist began to play, and a single haunting melody slowly wound its way across the keyboard and filled the hall. Anna Katz would soon get the recognition she deserved. The time had come to shed light on the truth of her life and music. Anna was about to be introduced to the world.

AUTHOR'S NOTE

I first learned about the role music played in concentration camps when I was a music student at the University of Wisconsin, Madison. One day I heard a recording of a haunting piece of music—Olivier Messiaen's "Quartet for the End of Time." I was amazed to learn that Messiaen had composed the entire piece in a concentration camp on half-broken instruments, the only ones available to him. It was unfathomable to me how anyone could write such beautiful music under such horrible circumstances, and I started reading about other musicians who had composed and performed in concentration camps.

The musical talent in Terezin included the likes of Gideon Klein, Viktor Ullmann, Hans Krasa, Pavel Haas, Rafael Schächter, and many others. Like the character by the same name in my book, Rafael Schächter was a vibrant musical presence in Terezin and conducted Verdi's Requiem numerous times. The composer that captures Emily's fascination, Felix Steinitz, is based on the composer Viktor Ullmann, and Steinitz's opera closely resembles Ullmann's astonishing piece "The Emperor of Atlantis."

The title of my book, *Sing What You Cannot Say,* is inspired by Schächter, Ullmann, and others who hid musical messages of hope and protest in their music. I have done my best to remain true to the historical details behind this story; any errors are entirely my own and unintentional.

The decision to refer to the concentration camp in this book as Terezin and not Theresienstadt was a difficult one and was based primarily on the following details: Terezin is the Czech name for what was originally a fortress city, while Theresienstadt is the German one.

The Nazis converted the fortress city into a ghetto and concentration camp in 1940 and referred to it as Theresienstadt. I also found that many letters, manuscripts, and interviews with survivors frequently referred to the camp as Terezin. On a personal note, I also felt that the name Terezin was a better literary choice because it represents one of the main themes in the book: encrypting hidden messages of hope and protest. Just as musical notes can represent hidden messages, so too can the choice of the original Czech name reflect a message of courage and hope: Terezin has always been our city; it will never be yours.

Acknowledgments

Thank you, Sarah Disbrow, for your thoughtful attention to detail and practical advice throughout the process of self-publishing this book. To my editor, K. Adams, your keen eye for language and story detail made this a much better book.

I am grateful to my entire family for believing in me and my ability to put this story to paper. My dear sisters and mother, you have always believed in my ability to do anything I have chosen to do. Thank you for never questioning the craziness of some of my choices. My husband, Peter, you have never once wavered in your support and conviction that I could do this—even when I myself was unsure, you somehow knew it was possible. My brilliant and adventurous children, Felix and Lena, you show us every day that absolutely everything is possible if you set your mind to it. Finally, my steadfast dogs, Oskar and Charlie—thank you for listening to all the versions of my story, for offering your quiet support, and for taking long walks in the woods with me as I worked through the details of the plot.

Printed in the United States
By Bookmasters